IF WE FALL

(CORRUPTED LOVE #3)

K.M. SCOTT

Books by K.M. Scott

If I Dream (Corrupted Love #1)
If You Fight (Corrupted Love #2)
If We Fall (Corrupted Love #3)

Crash Into Me (Heart of Stone #1)
Fall Into Me (Heart of Stone #2)
Give In To Me (Heart of Stone #3)
Heart of Stone Volume One Box Set
Ever After (Heart of Stone #4)
A Heart of Stone Christmas (Heart of Stone #5)
Unforgettable (Heart of Stone #6)
Unbreakable (Heart of Stone #7)
Heart of Stone Volume Two Box Set

Temptation (Club X #1)
Surrender (Club X #2)
Possession (Club X #3)
Satisfaction (Club X #4)
Acceptance (Club X #5)

SILK Volume One
SILK Volume Two
SILK Volume Three
SILK Volume Four

Books by K.M. Scott writing as Gabrielle Bisset

Blood Avenged (Sons of Navarus #1)
Blood Betrayed (Sons of Navarus #2)
Longing (A Sons of Navarus Short Story)
Blood Spirit (Sons of Navarus #3)
The Deepest Cut (A Sons of Navarus Short Story)
Blood Prophecy (Sons of Navarus #4)
Blood Craving (Sons of Navarus #5)
Blood Eclipse (Sons of Navarus #6)
The Sons of Navarus Box Set #1
The Sons of Navarus Box Set #2

Stolen Destiny (Destined Ones Duology #1)
Destiny Redeemed (Destined Ones Duology #2)

Love's Master
Masquerade
The Victorian Erotic Romance Trilogy

2017 Copper Key Media, LLC
Print Edition

Published in the United States
ISBN-10: 1-941594-56-5
ISBN-13: 978-1-941594-56-8

Cover Design: Natasha Snow Designs
www.natashasnowdesigns.com

Adult Content: Contains graphic sexual content

If We Fall

If we fall…

Ryder
I've protected Serena from everything I could in her father's world, but with each horrible act he committed, I knew the time would come when protecting her wouldn't be enough. When that day comes and it's either Robert or me who survives, I will do what I have to so the woman I love and my child are safe.

May heaven help me.

Serena
Every day I grow stronger as the child Ryder and I created grows inside me. I'm no fool, though. I know my father will do everything in his power to keep his control over us. But I'm not that scared little girl I used to be anymore, and the time is coming when he will realize that.

We're fighting for even more than love now. This time, we're fighting for family.

Corrupted Love Trilogy Playlist

Make You Feel My Love—Adele
Criminal—Fiona Apple
Comfortably Numb—Pink Floyd
Pillowtalk—Zayn
You Must Love Me—Madonna
All I Want Is You—U2
Love Me Like You Do—Ellie Goulding
The Difficult Kind—Sheryl Crow
In The Air Tonight—Phil Collins
Back In The Saddle Again—Aerosmith
Only The Young—Journey
High Enough—Damn Yankees
Wrapped Around Your Finger—The Police
Hanging By A Moment—Lighthouse
Touch, Peel and Stand—Days of the New
It's All Coming Back To Me Now—Celine Dion
Heavy—Collective Soul
Gimme Shelter—The Rolling Stones
At Last—Etta James
Diogo Piçarra—História

Chapter One

Ryder

I HEAR THE FAINT SOUND *of someone playing a piano off in the distance, and I lift my head to figure out where it's coming from. I'm in my rooms at the estate, so I guess the music is coming from outside. Walking down the steps, I hear it grow louder. It sounds happy, like the person playing the notes is enjoying every time their fingers hit the keys. The tune is familiar, but for the life of me, I can't place it.*

As I reach the bottom of the stairs and turn toward the back of the house, the final notes of the song play and I finally figure out what it is. The wedding march or whatever they call that music that plays when the bride walks down the aisle toward the altar.

Who's getting married?

I hurry toward the garden and turn the corner of the house to see a crowd of people standing in front of wooden folding chairs, all staring forward toward a gazebo I don't remember ever seeing before on the estate. A woman stops in front of it and a man reaches out his hand to take hers.

Who is he? I've never seen him at the estate before. I look around to find a familiar face and see Robert at the back of the crowd looking pleased at what is about to happen. No one else seems happy, though. None of the guests are smiling, and even the groom looks miserable.

Walking over to where Robert is standing, I ask, "What happened to Charles?"

He turns his head slowly and that crocodile grin of his spreads across his face. "It's not Janelle getting married, Ryder."

Panic rushes through me as I stand there waiting for the groom to raise the bride's veil. I watch as his face morphs into Robert's face. Horrified, I shake my head in disbelief. He promised he wouldn't do this to her.

"No! You swore you wouldn't marry her off to anyone else. You gave your word."

Robert simply shrugs, all the while grinning that infuriating smug smile. "There are consequences to everything, son. You know that."

"Who is he? Why does he look just like you?" I ask, my heart racing as the minister begins the ceremony.

"He's my new son to replace you, Ryder, so of course he's going to look like me. If you had done what I wanted, you'd be standing there with her and

you'd look like me."

"Don't do this! Don't make her marry him. I'm right here. I'm the baby's father, so she should be marrying me."

He shakes his head, still smiling, as all the men turn around to face us. They slowly begin walking toward me as they reach out to grab my arms.

"You won't be around, so someone will have to take your place, son. You knew this. You knew there would be consequences to your actions."

The men close in around me just as I watch the bride's veil being lifted. Serena looks back toward me with that same sad look in her eyes she had that first night I met her, and my heart breaks as I avoid her gaze to see how her wedding dress hangs over her pregnant belly.

"No! Don't let them do this, Serena! Run away! We can still be together."

Hands claw at me, tearing me in pieces, and as I begin to disappear, I hear her cry out, "Ryder, don't leave me here alone! You promised you'd protect me! Why did you lie?"

I didn't lie. Just run away and I'll find some way to get to you.

Slowly, I opened my eyes and looked around, but nothing looked familiar. I tried to sit up, but a jolt of pain shooting from my left shoulder and down my arm stopped me cold. Beads of sweat broke out on my forehead as I tried to handle the pain that quickly pushed out all the other thoughts in my head, like where the fuck was I?

After a few minutes, I could focus again, so I tried once more to figure out what was going on. Wherever I was, the room was colorless. White walls. White drapes on the windows. Was I dreaming?

My eyes fluttered shut, but I didn't want to sleep anymore. I didn't want to have that nightmare ever again. I didn't know where I was, but I knew Serena wasn't there with me, and I had to find out why.

Trying once more to sit up, I pushed past the excruciating pain and lifted myself off the bed. The sound of metal knocking against metal startled me, and I looked down to see my right arm handcuffed to the railing on the side of the bed.

What the fuck?

"Mr. Rhodes, I think you'll find you can't leave, although in your condition, you probably shouldn't go anywhere."

I turned to see a man dressed in a dark blue police uniform standing near the window smiling. He looked way too happy to be there talking to me.

"Why am I handcuffed to the bed?" I asked as my mind started to clear from the fog of whatever I'd been given.

"Because you're under arrest."

I didn't bother asking for what. I'd done enough in the years I'd worked for Robert to be arrested a dozen times over for more than a few crimes. Whatever they thought I did, I probably did it.

But I didn't care because now that I was wide awake the only thought in my mind was about Serena.

"Where is she? Is she okay?" I asked the stranger staring at me intently.

"Who?" he asked in a voice that said he didn't really care who I was talking about.

"Serena. She's pregnant. What happened to her?"

I moved to swing my legs off the bed, but whatever drugs they pumped into me made the room swim around me and I fell back onto the bed. Pain shot through my shoulder again, but I didn't have time to be lying around. I had to find Serena.

"Whoa! You're not going anywhere, buddy," the officer said in his authoritarian tone. "Just lay back and relax."

He tried to hold me down, but I needed to find out where Serena was and if she was okay. What the fuck about that didn't this guy understand?

"I need to see her. Where is she? Is she okay? For fuck's sake, she's pregnant with my child. I need to see her!"

The guy gave up trying to hold me down and ran

out of the room as I struggled to stand through the haze the painkillers. I put my feet down on the cold tile, which startled me for a moment, and lifted myself from the bed only to feel the metal tug on my wrist remind me that no matter how much I wanted to get the fuck out of this room, I wasn't going anywhere.

Well, unless I ripped the railing off the bed.

Bracing myself for the pain I knew would surely come, I yanked my arm up hard away from the bar and succeeded in doing not a damn thing. Well, except for making my shoulder feel like someone was burning through it with a red hot poker.

One of Maryland's finest and a few of his friends in police uniforms returned just in time to overreact to my attempted escape and force me back into the bed. Holding my hands up in surrender, I hoped none of them were trigger happy.

"I'm not trying to get away, guys. I'm just trying to find out where the mother of my child is and if she's okay. I just want to know she's all right."

A second guy as uptight looking as the first shook his head. "Just relax. You're not going anywhere."

Frustrated, I tried to keep my temper under control but all I wanted to do was fucking scream. "I get that. I just want to know she's okay. Is that too much to ask? Can't someone find out if Serena

Erickson is here, wherever here is, and if she's all right? I'll do whatever you want me to do if you can just find out."

Nobody answered any of my questions, and before I could start begging to know if Serena was okay, they filed out of the room, leaving me lying in that bed alone and terrified that the woman I loved was hurt.

Or worse.

A young nurse with sympathetic brown eyes that reminded me of Serena's came in to check on me. Her nametag said Katie and with a smile, she asked, "How are you feeling, Mr. Rhodes?"

I looked down at my arm handcuffed to the bedrail and sighed, letting the air out of my lungs with a loud whoosh. Looking up at her as she checked on my shoulder, I stared into her dark eyes and pleaded with her. "I'm okay, Katie, but I want to know if my girlfriend is okay too. Can you please find out for me?"

She turned away, fixing her gaze on my arm, and shook her head. "Aren't you concerned about your injury?"

I quickly glanced down at where her fingers gently pressed on the bandage. "No. It doesn't seem to be life threatening, so not really. I just want to find out if Serena is okay. She's pregnant, Katie. She was there when I got shot, and I don't know if she's okay.

I just want to know if she and the baby are safe. Can't you find out for me?"

She turned her head to look toward the door and then back at me. "I don't want to get in trouble."

"I don't want you to either. I just want to know if she and the baby are okay. That's it. Can you please find out for me?"

Katie nodded and hurried out into the hallway. I waited as my memory of what happened slowly came back to me. I shot first and then Jesse got a shot off before he fell. I'd been hit in the shoulder, so maybe that meant Serena hadn't been hurt.

I could only pray to God that she and the baby were okay.

The door opened again, and Katie hurried over to the side of my bed. Pretending to fix something on my bandage, she whispered, "She's down on the maternity floor. She's in labor right now. That's all I could find out."

Even though I was handcuffed to the bed, likely charged with murder for Jesse's death and shot in the shoulder, I couldn't help but smile. Our child was coming.

"Thank you."

Katie smiled and let her gaze drift down my body. "Did you really do what they said you did?"

"What did they say I did?"

She looked up at me and winced. "They say you

killed someone."

I thought about how true those words were and not just now. But of everyone I'd ever killed, Jesse was the one I truly regretted. I never wanted to hurt him. I didn't have a choice. There was no way I could let him hurt Alita any more than I could let him hurt Serena.

"Was it to protect her? Serena, the woman who's having the baby?" Katie asked, wide-eyed as she waited for me to answer.

Nodding, I admitted the truth to her, a perfect stranger. "I would do anything to protect her. She's everything to me."

Katie smiled and gently patted my forearm as she turned to leave. "She's one lucky girl. I hope things work out for you two."

As the door slowly closed behind her, I closed my eyes and hoped they did too.

I'm here, Serena. I might not be there next to you, but I'm close by, so don't worry. You're strong enough. You can do this.

AN HOUR PASSED and then two as I sat in that room alone waiting for any news about Serena and the baby. The guys in the uniforms stayed out in the hallway, and every so often, one of them pressed his nose to the thin pane of glass in the hospital room door to check if I was there.

Not that I was going anywhere. The handcuffs around my right wrist made sure of that.

I tried not to let the thought in, but the reality that I might never see Serena again or get to meet my child floated into my brain. I couldn't think that way. Yes, I'd have to pay for what I did, but I had to believe I'd see her and the baby sometime soon.

I wouldn't be able to go on living if I didn't believe that.

After nearly three hours, my mind began to turn on me. Maybe I would never get to meet my son or daughter. A murder charge wasn't something that was just going to go away. I'd done a lot of bad things. Maybe now I'd finally have to pay for all of them.

My chest tightened at the idea of missing out on everything we'd always dreamed of. No house in the mountains. No yard for a dog and our kids. No happiness in the end.

As I sat there in my misery playing out an empty future without Serena, the door opened and in walked two new Maryland State troopers and Robert. One officer stood at the foot of my bed while the other came around to the right side and stopped where my arm lay on the bed.

"What's happening?" I asked him as panic began to race through me.

Were they going to take me away before I had

the chance to even see my son or daughter?

The man lifted my arm and unlocked the handcuffs that had kept me attached to the bedrail. Letting my hand fall to the bed, he unfastened the cuffs from the rail and looked down at me.

"You're free to go, Mr. Rhodes. It isn't murder if you're defending someone. At least not a crime we can keep you in custody for."

I looked from one officer to the other and then to Robert, in shock at what I'd just heard. They weren't charging me for Jesse's death?

The two troopers filed out silently, leaving just Robert standing there staring at me. He cocked one eyebrow and shook his head. "Floyd was right. Fate loves you, son."

I'd never understood what the hell either of them saw that made them think fate even liked me in any way, but now wasn't the time for that discussion. Scanning the room for my clothes, I saw my pants and shirt on a chair in the corner, so I swung my legs out of the bed quickly and stood up.

But the drugs still coursing through my body made my head spin, so I sat down hard on the bed to get my bearings. "Robert, I need my clothes. I need to get dressed and get down to Serena before she has the baby."

He said nothing but handed me my things. I dressed as quickly as I could, easing my left shoulder into my shirt as pain pulsed from my wound and my heart raced. I'd finally get to see Serena and meet our child for the first time, just like she and I had planned.

Well, not just like we'd planned. We'd had something better in mind when we thought about welcoming our first child into the world, but no matter. I might be a little late, but I'd get there and be by her side when it counted.

I stood up from the bed, slower this time, and even though my legs felt shaky, I didn't have the time to get all of my strength back. Serena needed me, so weak or not, I had somewhere to be.

A date with destiny.

HURRYING TO THE NURSES' station on the maternity floor, I leaned over the counter and said, "I need to find Serena Erickson. She's in labor. I'm the father."

I looked back at Robert standing behind me and then looked back at the nurse staring up at me. "I mean, not her father. I'm the baby's father, and I'd like to be there when he or she arrives."

Although I guessed it didn't matter, I wasn't making much sense. I didn't care. She got the gist of what I meant. I'd let Robert explain it to her.

The nurse pointed down the hall and smiled. "She's in Room 308 and resting comfortably, Mr. Erickson."

The sound of that hit my ears completely wrong, and I cringed at her mistake. "Ugh, no…but thanks."

I left Robert to correct her and headed down to Serena's room. Resting comfortably probably meant they'd given her something for the pain, so maybe that had slowed things down to give me time to get there before the baby arrived. As my mind raced with a million questions, I tried to remind myself that women gave birth every day. She'd be fine.

We'd be fine.

Outside her room, I stopped and closed my eyes, trying to quiet my brain. Serena needed me to be calm and strong. What I always was for her. That's what she needed, so I took a deep breath and slowly pushed the door open, hoping I could be that for her.

"Ryder! You're here!"

My eyes fixed on Serena smiling and holding something in her arms. I took two steps into the room and stopped at the foot of her bed.

"He's here already? How? What happened? When did you go into labor?" I asked, unsure what to say as confusion, disappointment, and joy mixed together in my mind.

She beamed a smile and nodded. "He is. I guess when all that happened with Jesse, my labor started. I'm okay, though. Come look at him. He's the most perfect thing I've ever seen in my life, Ryder."

I stepped toward her and stopped dead as the realization of what I was seeing sunk in. "It's a boy?"

Serena reached out and took my hand in hers. "He is, and he's so beautiful. I can't stop looking at him. He's perfect in every way."

She lifted him slightly so I could see his face, and I stood there speechless staring at him there in her arms. So tiny, his little head was covered in dark hair and he had the tiniest mouth I'd ever seen on a human being. And the tiniest nose.

"Isn't he incredible?"

I wanted to say he was the most beautiful thing I'd seen in my life, but all my brain could do was tell my eyes to stay on that little face. His little face.

My son.

Serena squeezed my hand, pulling me out of my thoughts, and I looked down at her to see worry in her eyes. How could she be anything but blissfully happy with him there with her?

"What's wrong?" I asked as he made a little cooing noise and stretched his hand out from beneath the blanket.

"You weren't saying anything. I thought you weren't happy. Are you happy?" she asked, her voice trembling with fear.

Leaning down, I pressed a soft kiss to her lips and whispered against them, "I've never been happier in my entire life, Serena. Thank you."

Tears filled her eyes, and she smiled. "I didn't do this alone. Look what we did, Ryder," she said as she touched our son's perfect fingers. "He's got ten fingers and ten toes, and they're all soft and new."

Serena brushed her lips against his hand and giggled. "He even smells perfect. Wait until he opens his eyes. He's all you, Ryder."

I sat down beside her on the bed and kissed her on the cheek. "All us. Remember, we're in this together."

Turning to look at me, she nodded, smiling like I'd never seen her smile before. "The three of us. Ryder, Serena, and Cayden."

"Cayden?" I asked as I tried to remember that name being mentioned as one of the possibilities we'd talked about all those nights we lay in bed.

"Yes. Cayden. It means fighter."

Fighter. I didn't want my son to ever have to know what I'd done in my life before that moment. All the times I'd used my fists to hurt another person made me cringe now.

"Just as long as he never steps foot in the ring, Serena. I'll do whatever it takes to make sure he never sees that life."

Tilting her head, she kissed his forehead and whispered, "Welcome to the world, Cayden. You are wanted, and even more, you are loved."

Never before in my life had I gotten to

experience anything as beautiful as Serena holding our son and telling him we loved him. But one thing about this wasn't perfect, and I needed to change that.

"Serena, will you marry me?"

She snapped her head around to face me with a look of surprise. "Marry you?"

"Yes. Marry me. Our son deserves for us to be married."

"What about my father? He's never going to allow it, Ryder."

"I don't care what he allows. Do you love me, Serena?"

Nodding, she began to cry. "I've always loved you, Ryder."

Cayden opened his mouth to let out the tiniest little cry and then immediately fell back to sleep. I touched his cheek with my fingertip and turned to look at Serena. "And I love you, and now we have a son, and he clearly likes my idea enough to wake up and voice his opinion."

Serena bit her lip nervously. "Are you sure you want to marry me?"

I looked into those beautiful brown eyes so gentle and sweet and couldn't imagine life without her. "I've never been more sure about anything in my life, so say yes and we'll get married, and to hell with what Robert thinks about it."

"Okay. I want to marry you too."

Pulling her close, I kissed her and then kissed Cayden. "Good! I'll take care of everything and we'll do it as soon as we can."

Just as I explained our plans to her, the door opened and Robert walked in with Janelle right behind him. The two of them smiled like they were the new parents of our little boy, surprising me and Serena.

"I need to see that nephew of mine right now!" Janelle squealed as she came around the other side of the bed to see him.

"He's sleeping now, but here he is. Cayden Rhodes."

Janelle's eyes opened wide, and she stared down at the baby like he was something magical she'd never seen before in her life. "Oh, he's precious! I love him already, Serena. He's just the most wonderful thing I've ever seen!"

"Isn't he?" Serena beamed her pride at how perfect Cayden was. "I can't get over how much I love him and he's only been in my life for a couple hours."

Robert stood at the foot of the bed silently watching all of this until Janelle waved him over. He seemed reluctant to even be near the baby, but he slowly walked over to stand next to her and finally looked down at our son, studying him like he always seemed to be doing with me.

"He's a beautiful boy, Serena."

I expected him to say more, but I didn't expect him to take him out of his mother's arms without even asking. Instantly, my protective instincts kicked in, and I stood from the bed. I hadn't held my son yet, but Robert had before me.

He gently cradled Cayden in his arms, rocking him softly, but every part of my being stayed on edge as he held my son. He did nothing harmful to him and even smiled a few times, but everything about the scene playing out in front of me felt wrong. I didn't want Robert anywhere near Serena or Cayden. They were gentle and good, everything he wasn't, and for him to touch any part of them sickened me.

Turning his back to the three of us, he walked around the bed and stopped next to me. As he handed my son to me, he whispered, "Someday you're going to grow up to rule the world, little boy. You've got a great future ahead of you."

I took the baby into my arms for the first time and breathed a sigh of relief as I held him close to me, ready to protect him from the likes of Robert if I had to.

Now and for the rest of his life.

Serena eagerly reached out to take him again, and I saw the worry written all over her face. She knew, like I did, we would have to protect Cayden from his grandfather and all his world.

Chapter Two

Serena

THE HUNGRY STARE in my father's eyes when he looked at my son terrified me, and everything my mother told me about his obsessions raced through my brain. I wouldn't let him do that to my child, and I knew Ryder would sooner die than see Cayden go through what we'd dealt with.

"I think our little boy is tired from all this excitement, so maybe he should rest," Ryder said as he sat down beside me again. "Mommy and baby need to recharge their batteries. It's been a big day for both of them."

He took my hand in his and gently squeezed it, like a sign that he'd seen that same possessive look in my father's eyes when he looked at our son.

"Can I come back and see him again?" Janelle asked in a voice filled with disappointment. Her pout looked genuine, but I had to admit that her affection for the baby surprised me. Never before had she shown any interest at all in anything regarding me.

As much as I may have wanted to say no because

I knew she'd come with my father in tow, I smiled up at her and nodded. "Sure. I think we'll be here for at least another day, so you can come later today or maybe be at the house when we get home tomorrow."

Janelle's face lit up with excitement, and she turned to look at my father. "You said my room was being turned into the nursery, right? Is that almost ready?"

Surprised to hear plans had been made without telling me, I turned to see Ryder grimacing at the whole conversation. It felt like every other time in my life when my father simply steamrolled over everyone and did exactly what he wanted, when he wanted.

"I just had them start last night, so it might be a few days."

Clutching Cayden to me, I couldn't help express my disgust with my father and his plans. "You have people working on our child's nursery without even asking his parents what they want the room to look like? Don't you think you should have at least consulted with us?"

My father's mouth dropped open and his usually staid expression slid from his face. For a moment, I thought my outburst had angered him, but he quickly put on a smile and lowered his head as if in deference to me.

"You're right, Serena. I should have asked you before getting the men to work. If you don't like anything you see when you return home, I will make sure they do things to your liking. For now, I think Janelle and I will leave you three alone. Janelle, let's go."

My sister hurried to follow my father as he turned on his heels and walked out of my hospital room, leaving Ryder and me speechless for a few moments. I'd never seen my father so contrite in my life.

"I don't think he expected you to call him out on that, Serena. He looked stunned," Ryder said proudly before kissing me on the cheek.

I looked down at Cayden and gently squeezed him to me. "Don't mess with mama bear."

Ryder chuckled at my comment and reached over to tickle the baby's cheeks. "Or daddy bear, for that matter."

"You know, I feel like a totally new person now. It's like this little angel came along and gave me the strength I've always wished I had. I didn't even think about what would happen if I said something to my father about that whole nursery thing. I didn't like it, and I said something about it."

He pulled me close and kissed the top of my head. "I'm proud of you, Serena. I want you to know that."

When he said things like that, I felt like I could conquer the world as long as I had him by my side. But I needed someone else with me too.

Looking up at him, I asked, "What about my mother, Ryder? Where is she? I want her to see her grandson."

The look of uncertainty settled into his face, worrying me. "Michael got her away, but I don't know anything more. I gave him your number to call, but then everything with Jesse happened…"

His sentence slowly faded away, and I heard in his voice the regret for what he'd had to do about his friend. Ryder may have had to do things most people would be appalled by, but it wasn't in his nature to be unnecessarily cruel.

He just didn't have a choice out there at my mother's house.

"You did what you had to so I wouldn't get hurt. Don't blame yourself. He made his choice when he agreed to do what my father ordered him to do."

Ryder stood from the bed and slowly walked toward the window. "I know. Luckily, the police don't blame me either, or I'd still be handcuffed to the bed two floors up."

"What?" I said far too loudly and sat up straight, waking Cayden in the process. "What happened?"

He looked back at me and shook his head. "Nothing worth talking about. When I woke up, I was under arrest for Jesse's murder. But everything got straightened out. Don't worry."

The baby began to cry, so I nestled him to my breast and began to feed him as the mere thought of Ryder being under arrest simply for protecting me made my heart hurt. "That's not right. You weren't trying to hurt him. You told him over and over to just leave and go back to my father. I'll tell the police that so they can know you didn't do anything wrong, Ryder."

"It's okay," he said, leaning against the window ledge as he watched me feed Cayden. "They did their investigation and figured out I was protecting you. It's okay now. Don't worry."

"I am worried, Ryder. No matter what my father looked like here today when he came to see the baby, he sent someone to kill my mother. I can't forgive that. I can't forgive anything he's done. Now that Cayden is here, everything's different. At least it is for me. I don't want our son tainted by that world my father lives in. I don't want that ugliness touching him."

"You don't know how much I wish I had gotten you away from all that before he was born, Serena. If only I hadn't screwed everything up," Ryder said quietly.

"I know, but that's all in the past. Now we have the three of us, our family, to protect. Our son can't afford for me to be weak not a day longer."

Ryder smiled and motioned toward where the baby lay happily eating. "There's nothing about this scene that looks weak to me. I wish I had been there for you when you were giving birth to him. I'm sorry about that."

I extended my arm toward him and he walked over to take my hand in his. "There's nothing to be sorry about. It was a birth like any other. You were there for the important part in the beginning and for this part," I said with a giggle.

He sat down next to me and tenderly ran his hand over the top of Cayden's head, touching his soft black hair. "I swear to you that we're going to be okay. This little guy has changed everything, and from now on, I'm not going to be doing anything for your father that I'd be ashamed if someday my son found out about it. That might mean we have some lean times ahead of us because I'm probably going to have to get a different job, but I'm not doing Robert's dirty work anymore."

The memory of my father so intently focused on Cayden made me think it would be highly unlikely he'd do anything to risk us leaving the house. Now that my mother was safely away, he had no real control over me anymore, so if he decided he couldn't abide by Ryder's choices, the three of us would leave that place, and I'd never look back.

"I don't think he'll give you a difficult time, to be honest. I'm more concerned about how interested he is already in our son. You saw how he talked to him, didn't you? It made the hair on the back of my neck stand up. He's always wanted a son, and I think for a long time he found that in you. Now I'm afraid he wants to find that in our son."

A hard look settled into Ryder's eyes, and he shook his head. "I wanted to tell him to get the hell out of here when he was talking to him. It's like I could see the wheels turning in his head the whole time he was looking at him. He's not getting his hands on him, Serena. I promise you that."

I lifted Cayden to my shoulder and gently patted his back to burp him. I loved the feel of him next to me, a tiny human entirely dependent on his parents for everything. That meant the world to me. I'd lived my entire life with a father who manipulated me emotionally and tried to control my every move-ment, and now that I was a mother, I knew just how terribly wrong that had been of him to do to me and Janelle. She never seemed to be bothered by it, but I'd always bristled against his controlling my life with an iron hand.

My son would never experience that misery. Not from me or Ryder, and not from my father. Whether Robert Erickson knew it or not, his world had turned on its axis. The days of him ruling over me were over.

"We're going to have to be careful, Serena. Your mother is right. When he fixes his focus on someone or something, he'll do whatever it takes to make sure he calls it his. It used to be you and then it was me. Now it looks like he's moved on to Cayden. But if he thinks he's going to take him away from us, I won't hesitate for a moment. I want you to know that. I'll do what I have to."

Ryder took the baby in his arms to give me a little break, and I watched as he slowly walked around the room with his son. The joy in his eyes as he looked down at that tiny bundle cradled in his protective arms made my heart swell with happiness.

This was what Oliver had hoped we'd never have together. He'd taken it from us, but only temporarily.

And now that I had this in my life, I would protect it with everything in my being.

"You look so wonderful holding him," I said as Ryder smiled down at Cayden.

He looked at me, and I saw tears in his eyes. "You know, I wasn't sure anyone like me should even be a father, Serena. I never doubted you'd be a wonderful mother. You're sweet and gentle and everything a child could need. But I'm hard and I've done things that I'm not proud of. I didn't know if I could be what a father needs to be."

His doubt tugged at my heart. I'd never for a second thought Ryder wouldn't be a wonderful father. Protective and strong, he was everything I'd always wished my father would have been for me.

"I knew you'd be a natural at it," I said as he bent his head to place a kiss on Cayden's cheek. "You're just what our son needs. I hope you know that."

When he looked at me, I knew he didn't know that at all. "I just want to be someone he can be proud of. Someone you're proud of. I've done a lot of things in my life that I'm not proud of, Serena. I never want to look into his eyes as he asks me why I did them because I don't think I could handle admitting the truth."

I hated seeing the man I loved like this. What he'd done tortured him. He didn't sleep like he should because he was up tossing and turning every night at the regret he felt. And more often than not, the only solace he found was in a bottle of whisky. Nothing I could say seemed to affect him.

"You did what you had to so you could survive. So you could protect his mother. I know how much you hate the things you've done, but our son's birth gives us a fresh start. Take it. I am. I see his birth as the day I begin my life over. I'm not someone's daughter now. I'm Cayden's mother. Let it do the same for you. You're not my father's employee or the one he uses to exact his revenge. You're Cayden's father, and that's more important than anything you've ever done before this moment."

He smiled, but I knew his torment remained, even if on the outside he looked happy. I hated my father for what he'd done to Ryder. He'd set out to tear us apart, and when he couldn't do that, he did all he could to break him.

But Ryder was too strong for him. He wouldn't become the monster my father wanted him to be, even though on the inside, he lived with those regrets, and nothing could change that.

Things were different now. Bringing a life into the world did that, and as I watched him with our baby, I believed he would someday put all that ugliness my father had forced on him behind him.

We'd be happy just like we always dreamed we would. I had to keep believing that one day we'd be free of Robert Erickson's world and everything it forced us to do.

Ryder handed Cayden to me and sat down on the bed beside me. Putting his arm around the two of us, he whispered, "I just told him how incredible his mother is. I think he understood because he looked at me like he knew what I was talking about."

I turned to look into his green eyes that had enchanted me from the first moment I gazed into them and smiled. "Well, his father is pretty incredible too, and I'm going to make sure he knows that."

"While I was walking with him, I was thinking about how this all started between you and me. How I'd see you staring at me around corners, looking at me with those big brown eyes like I was something you couldn't figure out but wanted to. I never told you this, but from that first night, I couldn't stop thinking about you because of how disappointed you looked when you met me."

"I wasn't disappointed because it was you. I just had hoped my father would have found my mother that night. Please don't think it was because of you that I looked that way."

Ryder shook his head and smiled. "I don't. But I couldn't forget how unhappy you looked that night. I didn't even know you, but it bothered me to think you were sad about something, even though I knew had nothing to do with me."

"That's because you're kind. You don't think you are because you've had to be so brutal for so long, but I saw it in your eyes the first time I went to your room."

"Only with you. The rest of the world sees only the hardness, but I don't care what the rest of the world thinks of me. All I care is what you and our son think."

His voice cracked as he said those words. I didn't care what the rest of the world thought of Ryder either. They could think whatever they want. That he was a barbaric fighter. That he was a dangerous thug.

That he was that junkyard dog my father wanted to think he was.

None of these things were who he was. They were who he had to be to survive, first as a teenager thrown into The Pit by his uncle and then as a man forced to be one of my father's men. He'd done what he'd had to do. Anyone would in his situation.

But I knew the man he truly was. The protector. The savior who brought me back from death and each time made me see that I had something to live for.

Cradling his face in my palm, I felt the stubble on his jaw pricking my skin. "You're a good man, Ryder. Someday when all of this is over and we aren't fighting to survive in this world of my father's, you'll have the chance to be that man all the time. Until then, you're the reason I'm alive and our son exists. There's no more good in the world than that to me."

Ryder rested his head on my shoulder and sighed. "I can't wait for that day. I hope Cayden isn't too old by that time and hasn't seen what goes on in your father's world by then."

I looked down at the baby and felt completely content surrounded by the men in my life I loved more than anything else in the world. But I wasn't ruling out adding to our family sometime in the future.

"Maybe he'll have a baby sister or brother by that time too," I said quietly, unsure of Ryder's feelings on the idea.

I wouldn't blame him if he hadn't thought that far into the future, but having Cayden had ignited something inside me, and I loved the idea of us having a big family someday.

"A baby sister or brother? You just gave birth, Serena."

Turning to face him, I searched his face for disapproval at my suggestion, but I didn't find any. Just surprise.

"I know, but it wasn't too bad and we have this wonderful little boy now, so I just thought maybe when we get the hang of what to do with him, we might want to have another. Or a few more others," I said tentatively, hoping not to scare him half to death.

A sly smile spread across his lips, and he got that sexy look in his eyes I always loved. "A few more, huh? I guess I don't have a choice. If that's what will make you happy, we're just going to make more just like him."

I kissed him softly on the lips and pressed my forehead to his. "There are definitely worse things in life than what we have to do to make children, right?"

"Definitely. I can think of a million things worse than having to make love to the woman I adore," he said playfully.

"Do you really adore me?" I asked, suddenly needing reassurance about how he felt about me.

Ryder leaned back away from me and knitted his brow, like my question upset him. He cradled my face in his hands and stared deep into my eyes as if what he needed to say were the most important words he'd ever utter.

"I didn't mean to question—"

"You're everything to me, Serena. You have been since the moment I realized I loved you. I wouldn't want to go on living if I didn't have you by my side. You're the reason I wake up in the morning and want to go on after everything I've done. You make me believe I can be a better man than I have been. You've given me the greatest gift anyone could ever hope for."

I smiled and looked down at our son sleeping in my arms. "A son?"

Ryder shook his head. "No. I'm not your father, Serena. I never needed a son. And I love him as much as I love you, but the gift you've given me is your love. You showed me love that I hadn't felt since my parents died, and you have no idea what that meant to me. Your love is the greatest gift I could ever hope for."

"I didn't have a choice," I whispered against his lips before kissing him. "I would have had to be crazy not to fall in love with you."

He kissed me and then leaned down to kiss Cayden, and for at least a little while, we were the happiest parents in the world. As long as we were away from my father's world full of ugliness and uncertainty, we could enjoy the love we shared for each other and our son.

But I knew that might be short-lived because when we returned to the estate, once again all that my father forced on everyone around him would threaten the very happiness we enjoyed. I couldn't let that happen again, though.

We had too much to lose now.

Chapter Three

Ryder

EVEN THOUGH I would have preferred to stay at the hospital with Serena and Cayden, I headed back to the estate to clean up since I smelled like a combination of day old sweat and the sickly odor of my dressing needing to be changed on my shoulder. Dread filled me as I drove through the front gates, making my stomach twist into knots because no matter how Robert acted at the hospital, the truth was he had sent Jesse to kill Alita.

And my stopping Jesse made me a problem he'd deal with. Sooner or later.

I snuck around the main house and up the stairs into the apartment, happy to avoid dealing with any of Robert or his men today. All I wanted to do was clean up and return to my family waiting for me in that hospital room. I didn't need some confrontation with him that couldn't end well.

What he'd ordered Jesse to do sat like an elephant between us, but neither of us had mentioned a word about it at the hospital. I didn't know how to express my hatred for what he'd tried to do to Alita or how he knew killing her would crush Serena but ordered it anyway. I'd expected to see some rage from him when he first saw me that day, but he'd pushed that down inside for another time, no doubt.

Robert never let his disappointment stay a secret for very long, though.

I expected to suffer the consequences of my actions at any moment, so my guard was up as I walked back to the car to return to the hospital. I didn't know when or how, but I knew he'd make me pay for disobeying him.

Just as I reached the bottom of the stairs outside the apartment, I heard a deep voice behind me say, "Mr. Erickson needs to speak to you."

I didn't recognize it, and when I turned around, I saw a stranger standing just outside the door leading to the main house. He wore a black suit like all of Robert's men did, and the telltale bulge under his jacket told me he was armed. Younger than me, he had a hard look to him and I wondered where Robert had found this one. Had he brought him from the fight circuit like he did with me? The way the guy stood made me think he'd fought somewhere before.

"Tell him I'll talk to him when I come home from the hospital."

The man took two steps toward me and reached into his jacket to give me the sign that my answer wasn't the one he'd wanted to hear. Scowling, he shook his head. "He needs to speak to you now."

The bullet hole in my shoulder made me want to avoid getting into another gunfight with one of Robert's men, even if I thought I could probably wound this new guy and put him in his place. I might not have been the golden boy anymore, but I wasn't just another of his men either.

Turning around, I walked toward him and stopped just before I passed by. I looked him straight in the eyes and smiled. "Somebody needs to give you a rundown of who's who around here. You obviously know my name, but you don't know who I am. I suggest you find out fast before you get hurt."

He turned to look at me, stunned for a moment by my implicit threat, and then narrowed his eyes to slits. "I know who you are. I've heard all about you."

"Then be careful with how you talk to me."

I didn't bother to wait for him to reply since I didn't give a fuck what he thought and walked into the main house to answer Robert's summons. While I didn't appreciate his man's attitude, I hated that Robert still thought he could just demand to speak to me or Serena any damn time he wanted to and we were expected to come running.

By the time I reached his office, I was seething

and in no mood to deal with the inevitable discussion about what had happened out at Alita's house. But better to get it out of the way once and for all. I just hoped he didn't plan on beating the hell out of me again because my injured shoulder wasn't going to be able to handle that kind of attack for a while.

I stopped outside the door just as I had after he'd had his guys beat me senseless and waited to be told I could come in because no matter what he seemed like at the hospital, Robert didn't forgive betrayals and once again, I'd gone against his wishes.

Now it was just a matter of the punishment.

Unlike before, I didn't fear what he'd do to Serena. I couldn't put my finger on it, but something felt different now, like her giving birth to a son had improved her standing in his eyes. That even someone barely educated like me knew she wasn't responsible for that didn't matter. He just seemed to look at her differently now.

She'd accomplished something he thought of as worthy, so he finally saw her as worthy.

And while I didn't like the way he looked at my son like he had great plans for him, I didn't think Robert was the type of man to hurt a newborn. No, the one who would pay for this newest betrayal would be me.

I knocked softly on the doorframe, and he

looked over at me wearing one of those crocodile grins that still terrified me because I knew what they meant. Someone was going to be in a world of hurt soon, if his past behavior was any indication. Probably me.

"Ryder, please come in. No need to knock. This is your home. You're always welcome here."

Said the spider to the fly.

His smile and the tone of his words didn't match one another—a sure sign of a psychopath—but I braced myself for whatever might come next and stepped into his office. Two men around my size stood at their posts in front of the bookcase and another stood at the back of the room near the windows. None of them appeared to even care that I'd come in, so I relaxed a little and turned my focus to Robert sitting behind his desk.

"Your overeager new guy tells me you want to see me," I said with probably too much cockiness for my own good.

Behind me, I heard the man come into the room and stop at the door to take his position where I used to. I turned to throw him a glance to let him know I still didn't appreciate the way he'd talked to me outside and then looked back at Robert.

"So are we going to do this or not? I figure this time you might not stop at just a beating, but it seems shitty to take a newborn baby's father from him not two days into his life."

No matter how much bravado I stuffed into each word, inside I worried that Robert planned to do just that—take me from Serena and Cayden, and not just by sending me somewhere far away. That crocodile smile he wore even now made me think these might be the last breaths I'd ever take.

But if I was going out of this world, I planned to fight like hell before it happened. I had too much to lose now.

He stood from behind his desk, and I reached for my gun, knowing the four men surrounding me did the same. I didn't care that the odds were against me. If I could get off one good shot, at least Serena and Cayden wouldn't have to live under Robert's rule another day of their lives. My life for that was a trade I could accept.

Robert raised his hands as that smile slid from his face. "There is no need for guns, gentleman. Ryder, you're among family here."

I'd seen what his version of family meant. That's why I carried a gun.

He offered me a seat in front of him in one of those red leather chairs. "Please, sit down. This is a happy day for both of us."

Looking around, I saw the four men had returned to their jobs and weren't paying attention to us anymore. "A happy day? Are we talking about my son's birth or something else?"

"Sit, Ryder. Please."

I slowly lowered myself into the chair closer to the door and tried to look relaxed, but Robert's strangely happy mood confused me. I'd disobeyed him and betrayed him. There was no reason to believe he wouldn't exact his retribution for that.

The only question was when.

"How's that shoulder feeling?" he asked, smirking like he'd said something amusing.

At the moment, it felt like shit, but I didn't want to tell him that. Lifting my head, I braced myself for the pain and shrugged as if I wasn't recovering from a bullet entering my body.

"It's fine. Nothing that won't heal."

He gave me another smirk and moved on with the reason he'd summoned me. "I wanted to tell you how proud I am of both you and Serena. Cayden is a very lucky boy."

Robert nodded, like he wanted me to truly believe he felt that way. I didn't care what he felt about my family. All I wanted was for him to keep as far away from them as possible.

"Yes, my son is a very lucky boy. Is that what you wanted me to come here to talk about?"

"No. I wanted to inform you that you've been promoted."

I stared across the desk at him in shock.

"Promoted? What does that mean?" I asked as the possibilities of what he could mean tore through my brain.

To Robert, promoted likely meant something entirely different from what it meant to me. Tyrants often defined things very differently from the rest of the world.

"I'm making you head of security for the estate. You'll be over Johnson. Brace yourself for days filled with fishing stories," he said with a chuckle that didn't sound maniacal in the least.

Stunned, I tried to speak but nothing came out. Promoted to head of security? He wasn't going to punish me for not letting Jesse kill Alita? I couldn't believe it.

"So now I get something for betraying you? Best not to let these guys know about that. It's going to make keeping them in line hard."

Robert's eyes opened wide as a look of rage transformed his face into an ugly grimace, and he quickly waved the men out of the room. "Leave us alone. Wait for me to call you back in," he said gruffly.

They filed out without saying a word, leaving just the two of us sitting there like we had so many times before. But now something had changed between us.

He leaned forward toward me, steepling his

fingers in front of his face and staring over them at me. "You're full of surprises, son. I can't help but like that trait in you. Just when I think you're down for the count, you rise up like a phoenix. I'm convinced fate loves you, son."

Every time he called me son my stomach tensed up like my body expected a fist to hit it. I wasn't his son. I'd never been his son. And I sure as hell didn't want to be one of his children after seeing how he treated them.

"Fate, huh? I think it's simple science how boys are made, Robert."

A look of confusion settled into his face for a moment before he chuckled again. "No, I wasn't talking about our little guy. I meant how you got rid of your friend. I had a feeling you'd go out there after him. I didn't expect you to do what you did, though. That's love for you, though, right?"

I didn't know where Robert was going with any of this, but I didn't intend on denying anything. I didn't like what I'd had to do, but I hadn't put Jesse in that position. He did.

"Losing Alita would have killed Serena. You knew it and you still ordered her death. Just let her be."

He took a deep breath and sat back, crossing his arms over his chest. "So now my wife is in the wind with that son of hers. Oh, you didn't know Michael was her bastard child? The look on your face says she didn't tell you."

Shaking my head, I tried to conceal my surprise at Robert's bombshell. "I had no idea, but it doesn't change anything. I don't care what she did twenty years ago. I couldn't let Jesse kill her. I couldn't do that to Serena."

"I imagined you wouldn't. I just thought Jesse would be better at his job. But since he wasn't and you're still here, I have no choice but to make sure you're happy."

"Why? What do you care if I'm happy? And don't say that you know it would break Serena's heart if you killed me or even sent me away because you've never given a damn about her."

Robert shook his head. "I care because you've finally given me what I always wanted from you. That little boy is going to carry on this family. That's why I brought you here. I hoped you'd choose Janelle, but you didn't, so plans changed slightly. But in the end, the result was exactly what I always wanted."

So Janelle had been right. I had been brought to the estate as a stud after all.

"And you aren't just going to get rid of me now that Serena and I have produced an heir for you?"

He grimaced like the idea horrified him. "No. Our boy needs you to teach him. I'd be foolish to get rid of you now."

"My boy, Robert. My son. Cayden is my son, not yours. I'm not going to let you manipulate him like you've done to Serena and Janelle all their lives."

He brushed off my statements and returned to my promotion as if nothing else had been said. "You'll start in your new position in a few weeks. Johnson has been informed, and I suspect he's gathering his best fish stories as we speak."

"Why a few weeks?" I asked, on edge for anything that seemed out of the ordinary with him.

But he simply shrugged. "I wanted to give you some time with Serena and the baby."

I couldn't decide if he'd lost his mind or lost his edge. Either way, Robert was still a madman. Now he just seemed to be a madman who'd gotten what he wanted.

At least for the moment.

As with all madmen, his mood would change. Who would suffer when it did was what I didn't know. I suspected it would be Alita, if he could find her.

I intended on making sure he never did.

Standing to leave, I extended my hand to shake his. "Thank you for everything, Robert."

He stared at my hand for a moment and then grabbed it. "Usually, the handshake is saved for when the deal is closed. We aren't there just yet, son.

But for now, you're welcome."

I left without saying another word. All I knew was truer words had never been spoken. We weren't to the end of our business yet. I knew that for sure.

✧ ✧ ✧

"HAVE YOU SEEN the nursery yet?" Serena asked as I pulled the car up to the front of the house.

Putting the car in park, I turned to face her and shook my head. "No. I didn't want to spend any more time here than I had to after my meeting with your father and I wanted to get back to the hospital so we'd have time to hit the courthouse today."

Serena leaned toward me and kissed me softly on the lips. "I understand, husband. I wish we didn't have to come back here at all. But all that matters is the three of us are together, right?"

"Right. Let me come around and get you before I get Cayden."

I moved to open my door, but Serena stopped me. "I'm not an invalid, Ryder. I can get out of the car myself. I just had a baby. If anyone should be taking it easy, it's you. You were shot, remember?"

The ache in my shoulder never let me forget, but I didn't want her to know how bad it hurt, so I just smiled. "I'm fine, and I know you just had a baby, but let me take care of you, okay? That's not a request either."

She giggled in that sweet way I loved, and when I opened her door, she looked up at me with gentleness in her eyes and said, "I love having a husband who wants to take care of me, but he has to let me take care of him too. Remember the vows? Love, honor, and cherish. That means taking care of you too, Ryder."

"I remember, but that doesn't mean I'm just going to change who I am. So let's get you out of the car so we can get our son to his new room."

Her brown eyes clouded over with worry. "Let's hope it's not horrible. I have this vision of our son's room decorated in all gold with dollar signs all over."

Cringing, I shut the car door and hoped Robert had better taste than that. "Sounds like some kind of music mogul's bedroom."

I got Cayden out of the car and into Serena's arms, and the three of us walked up to those enormous glass front doors I remembered being impressed by the night I arrived at the estate. So much had happened since then. Now I wasn't just a stray being let into the house but the husband of one of Robert's daughters and the father of his grandson.

Things had definitely changed.

We walked through the entryway over the marble floor to the winding staircase and neither of us looked to our left as we passed Robert's office because our son held our complete attention. He had no idea how important that was as he slept safely in Serena's arms.

I opened the door to what had been Janelle's room and heard Serena inhale sharply behind me as we saw the changes her father had made for it to be Cayden's nursery. He'd obviously left the design to someone who liked babies. The walls had been painted a pale green and pictures of animals lined the entire room. Giraffes, lions, tigers, and zebras made the place look like a zoo.

"Oh, my God," Serena said quietly in my ear as we walked toward the dark wood crib at the far end of the room. "It's beautiful!"

I hadn't exactly thought of my son spending his first years in a zoo, but the design was cute for a baby. It certainly could have been much worse.

"This is your new room, Cayden," she said as she pointed toward the animals painted on the wall. "That's a zebra, and that's a lion. And that tall, spotted animal is a giraffe."

Seeing her so utterly content and happy made me want to think everything would be okay from now on. I knew that was unlikely, but as I watched Serena dote on our son in the middle of that room Robert had redecorated just for him, I had hope.

I wrapped my arms around her and the baby and whispered in her ear, "I think he might like it. Babies love animals, right?"

Serena smiled. "Actually, babies can't really see colors like these. That's why some people make their nurseries black and red since they can see those colors. But it means a lot, I think, that my father did this for Cayden and actually remembered he wasn't just a tiny adult. Don't you think so?"

I wanted to think so. I didn't want to ruin this moment for her either, so I nodded and pretended that I hadn't just heard Robert talk a few hours earlier about ordering Alita's death like he was commenting on the temperature of the room. He hadn't changed, and I had a feeling Serena knew it too. She just wanted to believe he had for Cayden's sake.

"It does mean a lot. I have something to tell you too."

For a moment, she looked concerned and drew her eyebrows in with worry. "Oh? Did something happen to my mother, Ryder?"

Shaking my head, I hurried to tell her the good news. "No, no. I'm sure Michael is keeping her safe. No, I wanted to tell you that Robert made me head of security for the estate. No more working as one of his men or fighting. I'll just be spending my days figuring out why that front gate camera never works right and listening to Johnson tell me boring fishing stories."

Her eyes lit up with happiness, and she leaned in

to kiss me. "Oh, that's great news! Maybe this is a sign of things to come."

As Serena placed Cayden down into his new crib and tucked him in under a pale green blanket, I wanted to believe things would be okay. Robert was a still a madman, but we'd changed. I wasn't that same person who'd walked through those glass front doors and worried he didn't belong, and Serena wasn't the same either. Having Cayden had made her stronger than ever before.

Maybe that would make all the difference.

Chapter Four

Ryder

*M*Y HANDS PUSH *hard to keep his head beneath the water as his arms and legs flail desperately to get free of my hold. It's no use. Better to let the inevitable end come sooner than later and suffer less. This is just the way it has to be.*

I watch as his movements slow and gradually stop altogether, his body going limp and sliding down the side of the hot tub until nothing but the top of his head shows.

And that is the end of Jacob Landon.

The bubbles still simmer across the water, and I stare into it for a moment before pushing down my sleeves. I completed the job. Now to get back to my life.

Turning to leave, out of the corner of my eye I see something move. I spin around and see Jacob Landon standing in front of me. His dark, wet hair sticks to his head, and his eyes bulge out of their sockets. His pale skin looks heavy and thick, like there's too much of it on his bones, and water seeps out of every part of him.

He opens his mouth to speak, but instead horrible choking sounds come out. Awful noises like his lungs are filled with liquid and no matter how much he coughs, he can't get it all out. I watch, expecting his face to turn beet red from coughing so violently, but he remains that sickly pale color.

Finally, he bends over the side of the hot tub and vomits so hard it sounds like something painful is being cast out of his body. I stand there in shock as the words repeat in my mind over and over.

He's dead. He can't be alive. I killed him.

Lifting his head, he sneers like he knows exactly what's going through my mind at that moment and my thoughts disgust him.

He points at me, water dripping off the tip of his finger slowly but steadily, and gurgles, "Yes, I'm dead, Ryder. You killed me. Just like Robert ordered you to."

I stare at him in horror, shaking my head as I watch water continue to pour out of him. "This isn't possible. You aren't standing there talking to me."

"Because you killed me. Yes, I know. I was just enjoying my nightly hour or so in my hot tub, and you drowned me. And for what? Because I called some girl a whore? I deserved to die for that?" he asks matter-of-factly.

I don't know if he deserved it or not. And I don't care.

"I'm not arguing with a dead man. You're dead. There's nothing more to say."

"And yet here I am and here you are, the man who killed me. I guess I should have seen this coming when I let Oliver marry Robert's daughter. I knew what he was and let that snake in anyway."

"Serena," I say to correct him, needing him to understand she isn't just Robert's daughter. She's Serena.

Staring at me with revulsion all over his face, he asks, "What?"

"Her name is Serena. Call her by her name."

He chokes out a mouthful of water that dribbles down his chin onto his chest and clears his throat as best he can. "Fine. Serena. I should have never let my brother get involved with Serena Erickson. I knew what she was and still let him marry her."

With every word, my rage threatens to explode out of me. I can't let him stand there and talk about her that way, like she's done anything to hurt anyone.

"You look upset, Ryder. What do you care what I think of your girlfriend? Whore or angel, what does it matter? She's Robert's daughter. That's all anyone needs to know."

"Shut the fuck up! Don't talk about my wife like that."

"Wife?" he asks wide-eyed, obviously surprised to hear Oliver isn't her husband anymore. "I guess that *means my brother isn't among the living."*

I simply shake my head, unwilling to defend myself to this fuck. I had a job to do and I did it. Period. Nothing more. Nothing less.

"You think that's how it is," he says like he knows what I was thinking. "But at some point, don't you think you have to accept some of the blame? I mean, you could have told Robert no when he started making you kill people."

"No. There was never any choice."

Water begins to pour out of his mouth and eyes, and I watch as he writhes in agony, trying desperately to stop it but failing. I reach out to help him, not knowing how I could but not wanting to see him suffer anymore, but I can't.

Nothing can help him.

When the water slows, he coughs violently until he can speak again. I keep expecting blood to come out, but always it's water. Water and more water.

"So never any choice. Did you think at all about killing me, or did it just happen like some robotic movement devoid of any emotion?"

I hadn't thought about it. Not really. Robert ordered me to do it, and after my surprise at hearing him actually say the words faded away, I felt nothing about killing Jacob Landon. Even now, as I stare at him, amazed at how much water still pours from his body, I feel little other than anger at how he's talked about Serena.

"I guess that means you're just some kind of killing machine. Nice. I could have used one of those when I was alive. Maybe if I thought to have Robert killed neither of us would be standing here tonight," Jacob says, sounding disappointed that he hadn't thought of the idea before that moment.

"You'll judge me for doing the same thing you just said you would have done?"

He ignores my attempt to show him his hypocrisy and takes a step forward in the hot tub. His eyes narrow to angry slits in his waterlogged head, and a gurgling noise comes from his throat that makes my blood run cold.

"He's evil, and you're just as bad. You're just like Robert! You are! You're no better, Ryder! No better! And you'll meet your end just like all of us you killed did, and no one will deserve it more!" he shouts, spitting water with every vicious word he spews.

I sat up straight in bed, my hands pushing the air in front of me to shield myself from the water he spit at me. Staring out in terror, I saw Jacob Landon wasn't in front of me anymore, and I was back in the bedroom I shared with Serena.

After my heart stopped slamming into my chest and I could take a breath, I shook my head to rid myself of the vivid nightmare. Never before since

Jacob Landon's death had I given him a moment's thought, but now what I'd done to him haunted me.

Was he right? Was I just as bad as Robert?

His claim that Robert would order my death just as he'd ordered Jacob's didn't surprise me, though. Ever since he found out about Serena and me, I'd prepared myself for the eventuality that he would get rid of me as he had so many other people he no longer saw a use for.

I ran my hand through my sweat drenched hair and reminded myself that I wasn't just some hapless business partner of his he could simply eliminate. I'd been the one who did his dirty work. I knew how he operated. I might not know when he'd come after me, but I could guess how.

Maybe the new cocky fucker who'd thought he could tell me what to do earlier that day would be the one to do the job. I already suspected he was more ego than brains or even brawn, so if he came after me, it would involve all sorts of talking and boasting before he did it. Just like those fighters who'd always thought the glaring and talking smack helped them, he'd find out while he was spouting his shit, I will have figured out a way to make him the one who got taken care of.

But maybe now that Cayden was born Robert wouldn't be in such a hurry to kill me, even after all I'd done to betray him. Maybe I wouldn't have to be that man I'd need to be to defend myself from him and his men.

I didn't want to kill anymore. I'd never wanted to. I knew people like Jacob Landon didn't believe me, but there never was a choice. Not with Robert. He made it clear every day. You either obeyed him or you paid with your life.

There was no middle ground. Those who obeyed were prized, and those who betrayed were punished.

As I sat there thinking about all I'd done, I knew Robert's strange obsession with me as his adopted son was the only reason I'd escaped real harm so far. Not even his daughter's love for me mattered as much. But a sick feeling in my gut told me I'd been replaced in his mind with someone else.

My son.

The sound of him sleeping in the room next to ours came through the baby monitor on the dresser, a mechanical reminder of the little human being who already had changed my life for the better in so many ways. Just the thought of Robert controlling Cayden's life like he'd controlled mine and Serena's made my stomach twist into knots. I wouldn't let him do that. I couldn't. Now that my son had come into my life, I swore I wouldn't kill again except to protect him and Serena.

I just feared that sometime in the future, I'd have to do just that to the very man who'd brought me here. If that happened, I would kill again. For them.

Serena shifted in the bed next to me, pushing her leg against mine, and I sat watching her for a moment. Still the sweetest and gentlest soul I'd ever met, even she'd grown harder in the past year because of what Robert had forced her to endure.

I touched her hair, so soft against my fingers, and wondered if we'd someday harden over so much that we became like Robert. Had Jacob been right?

Oliver sits at his desk, and I instantly notice how different he looks from Robert when he sits in his office. Surrounded by books, he seems dwarfed by them as he sits in his chair. I watch through the window as he swivels back and forth between those books of his positioned on either side of his desk as he researches something. I have no idea what it is, and I don't care.

I'm not there to discuss an appraisal with him. Tonight, I finally will put an end to him.

Swallowing hard, I push down every emotion inside me until one simple idea fills my mind. He must pay for what he's done to Serena and our unborn child.

I turn the door knob and find the front door unlocked. Cocky fuck. You threaten the daughter of the man who had your brother killed and you don't even lock the fucking front door? Mistakes like that are what cost people their lives.

Creeping down the dark hallway, I head toward the dim light coming from his office. I still have no idea how I'm going to do it. Do I torture him like I want to, beating him until there's nothing left to identify of that smug face of his? Do I just make it quick and shoot him twice in head? No talking, no build up, no nothing.

I don't know. Maybe when I'm standing in front of him remembering how I felt cradling Serena in my arms at the bottom of those stairs as our child died inside her I'll know then. What I do know is I want to do this one.

Only one of us can continue to walk the earth. Him or me. It can't be both.

I stop just before I reach his office door and pull my gun out of my waistband. I still don't know if I'm just going to shoot him, but in case he's armed, I need to be prepared.

Looking into the room, I see him working and wonder if he's already told Robert everything. Suddenly, a chill races down my spine. If he has, Serena could be in danger. I have to get back to the house to make sure she's okay.

Oliver doesn't move when I take a step into the room and stop, my gun pointed at his head. I take another step toward him, and then he looks at me. His beady little eyes open wide at the sight of me there with a gun in my hand.

"What are you doing here?" he asks in terror as his gaze darts from my face to the gun in my hand and back up to my eyes.

"You know what I'm doing here," I answer flatly, seeing no reason to explain the obvious.

His fear turns quickly to anger. "So have you and that slut wife of mine been planning this for long or is this because I planned to tell Robert everything tomorrow?"

Hatred courses through my veins at his mention of Serena like someone deserving of his insults, and I take a step toward him. "I'm going to enjoy doing this one."

I point my gun directly at the center of his forehead while he begins to beg for his life like a sniveling little pussy. "I don't have to tell him anything. I can just go away. It can be as simple as that. I just go away and you never have to deal with me again. Please. It doesn't have to be like this."

Rage makes my chest hurt, and I shake my head in disbelief that this fuck doesn't get it. "You pushed her down the stairs and left her for dead after you killed our child. Now you think you deserve some kind of fucking reprieve? What kind of reprieve did you give my child?"

He opens his mouth to speak but nothing comes out. Over and over, he looks like he wants to say something, but then he presses his lips shut. I watch and think he looks like some kind of fish I saw at an aquarium when I was a little boy.

"Nothing to say to that, Oliver? You pushed her down the stairs and kicked her. A pregnant woman and you kicked her. Why not just leave her?"

Shaking his head quickly left and right, he says, "I couldn't leave. Robert would have had me killed if I did that. I didn't have a choice."

His claim he didn't have a choice makes me want to kill him even more. "You didn't have a choice other than to try to kill your wife and kill her unborn baby?" I bellow at him, ready to see this end once and for all.

He raises his hands in surrender and continues to shake his head. "I didn't mean it like that. Please don't do this."

I don't say another thing and press the trigger on my gun, sending a single shot straight for his forehead. It hits him and he stops shaking his head no, slumping back against the chair.

The end of Oliver. A life for a life.

But as I stand there looking at the blood splatter behind him on the wall, he sits up and shakes his damn head again. How? He's dead. I saw him die.

"So now you can have her. Is that what this was all about?" he asks in a tone of disbelief.

"This isn't real," I say backing away. "You're

dead."

"Of course, I'm dead. You just shot me in the head," he says in that smart ass smug tone he's used with me before.

"I'm not doing this again with you fucking Landons."

"Doing what? Hearing the truth?" he asks as he wipes blood from around the hole in the center of his forehead.

"No. I'm not doing this with you too. You don't get to be self-righteous, you fuck. Maybe your brother has the right, but you don't. Not after what you did to Serena."

"Yeah, I was a shit to her, I guess. I never wanted to marry her, to be honest. My brother thought it was a good idea. He thought we could get some of the Erickson money by having me marry her. But that was never going to happen, was it?"

His casual way of talking about the woman I love pisses me off, but I know none of this is real. At least I think none of this is real. Fuck, I don't know. Maybe some of it is.

"I think he must know about you two, you know that?" Oliver says like he's enjoying our conversation and wants to keep it going. "I mean, now that I look back on it, it's hard to imagine anyone not knowing. You never could take your eyes off her whenever the two of you were near each other. Not that she was *innocent in all of this."*

Nothing he says means anything to me, so I turn to leave and am stunned to see him suddenly standing right in front of me. The hole where the bullet went in seems to be getting bigger and spreading across his forehead. I try to sidestep him, but he moves wherever I move, always shaking his head.

"I'm not going to say I'm sorry for killing you, Oliver. Don't bother trying to lecture me like your brother did. You got what you had coming to you."

He stops shaking his head, and for a moment, the hole doesn't get any bigger as he stares at me like my words bother him. "What do you have coming to you, Ryder? Now that you have what you've always wanted, what's it going to cost? Because nothing in Robert Erickson's world is free. So what's the price?"

I don't know what he means, but it doesn't matter. None of it matters.

"I'm not going away, Ryder. She may have forgotten me, but you won't. You're a killer, but obviously you aren't as cold as Robert thinks you are. Or you think you are. And you know your time is coming. He's going to get rid of you just like you got rid of me. When you become a hassle, your time's up," *he says with a grin as the hole in his head begins to spread again.*

His skin slowly disappears until all that's left of the top of his head is his skull and his brain. I raise my gun to shoot him point blank so I can at least stop him from grinning, but it doesn't work.

He just keeps smiling and repeating himself. "He's going to get rid of you like you got rid of me. He's going to get rid of you like you got rid of me."

Over and over, he says those same damn words until he's screaming at me in a terrifying, screechy voice. "He's going to get rid of you like you got rid of me, Ryder!"

I push past him to run out of the building as he continues to yell that again and again until.

"No!"

I sat up in the darkness, my heart pounding like a jackhammer in my chest and my mouth parched. It was all a dream.

"Ryder, what's wrong?" Serena asked quietly, placing her hand on my leg. "Did you have a nightmare?"

Struggling to get my bearings, I clutched her hand in mine and tried to figure out what the hell just happened. "I was talking to...I mean, I was having a dream about..."

She cupped my cheek with her hand and kissed me gently. "You're covered in sweat. Are you okay?"

Leaning into her palm, I closed my eyes and felt relief wash over me. "Yeah. It was just a nightmare."

"It's okay," she whispered against my lips.

"You're safe right here in bed with me. Why don't we lie down?"

I inhaled deeply and nodded while she eased me back onto the bed. Safe right there with her. Right where I belonged.

Fuck Oliver and fuck Jacob. They didn't know anything. I wasn't like Robert. I wasn't.

Serena rested her head on my chest and slowly ran her hand over my stomach. "Your heart is going a million miles a minute. That nightmare must have really gotten to you. Do you remember what it was about? Maybe talking about it will make you feel better."

I didn't know if I'd ever be able to forget my nightmares, but I couldn't tell Serena about them. She didn't need to be saddled with my guilt. I deserved it. She didn't.

Shaking my head, I felt her hair brush against my lips and reveled in her being there with me. "No, it's all just a blur now. I can't really remember anything that happened."

With fear in her voice, she asked, "Was it about the baby?"

"No," I answered truthfully, happy I didn't have to lie about that. I kissed the top of her head and said, "I'd remember that, I'm sure."

Serena sighed. "Good. I'm glad it wasn't about Cayden."

Tightening my arm around her, I pulled her body to mine until she melded to my side. "I'm sure it was nothing. Go back to sleep. I'll listen for him in case he wakes up."

"Okay. I love you, Ryder."

"I love you, Serena."

I listened as she drifted off to sleep, blissfully unaware of what I knew awaited me in my dreams. All I could hope was the man I tried to be now made up for everything I'd done before.

Chapter Five

Serena

EVERY NIGHT, RYDER tossed and turned next to me as we lay in bed, tormented by nightmares he refused to tell me about. Sometimes he woke up in terror, sweat pouring from him as he swung his arms like he was in the middle of a fight.

But I suspected it wasn't his time in the ring he dreamed about each night. Something darker troubled him, and I knew it had to do with what he'd done for my father, and if I was being truthful, for me. He hadn't killed Oliver for anyone but me.

Had I asked him for too much and now what he'd done haunted him?

He shook his head and mumbled, "No…I'm not like him…" Once and then twice he repeated those same words, and I watched as his expression turned down into a frown in his sleep.

Gently, I pushed on his arm to wake him up, unable to watch him like this. "Ryder, you're dreaming again. Wake up. Look at me."

Turning his head toward me, he opened his eyes

and smiled. "Are you okay?"

Such a typical Ryder reaction. Whatever he was dealing with, he hid it from me, and the first thing he thought of when he woke up was to see if I was okay.

"I'm fine. You were tossing and turning, and then you started talking in your sleep. I thought you might be having a nightmare."

He thought about my question for a moment and then shook his head. "I don't think so. Did I wake you up?"

Giving him a peck on the cheek, I felt his rough stubble against my lips. "Yes, but I'm more concerned about you than me waking up. Cayden wakes me up all the time. I've gotten used to it in the past month."

"Has it been a month already?" he asked with a smile before he nuzzled my neck, his stubble now tickling me.

I loved when he was like this. Sweet and sexy, as if whatever troubled him didn't exist and all he knew was happiness. All I wanted was for him to be happy. It's all I'd ever wanted for him.

"Ryder, aren't you tired?" I asked as he slid his hand up under my tank top to cup my breast.

Lifting his head, he gave me a sly smile and shook his head. "Not really. Sleep is overrated. Sex, on the other hand, is definitely not."

His lips trailed down my neck and slid across my

collarbone, sending shivers over my skin. Burying my hand in his hair, I held him to me and loved the sensations he created in me just with the merest touch of his lips on my body.

"What did you have in mind?" I asked with a giggle when he rolled over onto his back and pulled me on top of him.

His devilish grin told me the answer before he even said a word. Sliding his hands down to my hips, he gripped them tightly and held me on his cock. "I thought I'd fuck my wife until she couldn't walk anymore."

"And who will be taking care of our son after this fucking until I can't walk sex marathon is over? I bet you didn't think about that, now did you?"

Sliding his thumbs over toward my already wet pussy, he nodded. "I did think of that. I can take Cayden to work with me while you recuperate. See? I have this all planned out, so there's no use in fighting me."

I leaned forward and flicked my tongue along the seam of his mouth. "No fighting here. You sound like you have it all taken care of."

Ryder lifted his hips off the bed and ran his hard cock through my pussy. Grabbing my ass, he squeezed hard and moaned. "Good. I can't wait to be inside you, Serena."

He pulled me down on top of him and tugged

hard at my hair as he roughly spread my legs with his knee. A sweet ache formed in the pit of my stomach when he slid his cock over my clit, and the intensity in his eyes as he looked up at me made me whimper with need.

"Stop teasing, Ryder."

"I just love watching you get all excited for me," he said before he ran his tongue across his lower lip in that sexy way that made me want him all the more.

His playing frustrated me, and I pouted. "Not fair."

"Come here," he said as he pulled me to him and kissed me slow, his tongue gliding over mine and inching my desire up until I reached around and slid my hand over his cock.

"Somebody doesn't want to wait tonight. I like the way you feel wrapped around me like that. Don't stop."

"I've got a better idea," I said before I sat down on him and slowly let his cock fill me until there was no space left between us. Against his lips, I moaned, "Now that's better, don't you think?"

"Mmmm…I like this. Ride me, baby."

I lifted myself off him until just the tip of his cock stayed inside me and then rolled my hips slowly to take all of him. He slid his hands over my hips to my clit and traced circles over it with the pad of his thumb as I rode his cock. I watched him stare up at me with that look of pure desire that never failed to excite me.

The beginning of my orgasm began to uncoil inside me, and when it hit me, I slammed down on him, needing to feel him fill me completely. My thighs trembled against his sides while he watched me come, his gaze fixed on me like seeing how his cock pleasured me enchanted him.

"You looked like the perfect woman right at that moment when your cunt squeezed my cock at the end. Like all you ever wanted was me inside you."

Leaning forward, I kissed him and smiled against his lips. "I've always wanted you. You know that."

"Always, huh?" he said in a way that sounded like he didn't believe me.

I rolled my hips and felt him press against the inside of my belly. "Always."

His eyes twinkled at my answer, and he grinned wickedly. "I love when you say that."

He kissed me hard and rolled us over so he was on top of me. Flipping me onto my stomach, he pulled me up onto my knees and spread them wide. He slipped his hand around my throat and whispered in my ear in low voice that made me wet with desire, "I'm going to fuck you until you beg me to stop."

I pressed my hand against his cheek as he slid inside me. "I would never beg for you to stop."

"Then I guess this is how the rest of our lives go, right here with my cock buried inside you."

He pulled back, leaving me almost empty, and then thrust forward, filling me so completely I gasped for breath. Everything he was—strength, power, sensuality—washed over me, and I wanted more.

More of all he was. For the rest of my life. All he would be and everything I could be.

Ryder's hand tightened around my throat, and he grunted low and deep in my ear with every plunge into my body. Like every sound came from deep inside him in a place where that man who fought in the ring still existed.

His hand slid down over my breast and pinched my nipple, sending a string of need directly to my pussy. I pushed back as he rammed his cock into me, wanting to feel him find that place inside me that only he had ever touched.

"You're so fucking wet," he groaned in my ear before pinching my nipple again.

I loved when he said things as he fucked me. I rarely said anything, usually so lost in the feelings he created in me, but his words about how much he wanted me never failed to thrill me. He made me feel like I was his, like every part of me was his to protect and delight.

Gripping the sheets between my fingers, I reveled in the feel of him sliding in and out of me, faster and faster until his hard body slammed against my ass and pushed me forward with every thrust. He held my hips tightly, his fingertips sinking into my flesh, but I didn't care. Every sensation, whether it be pleasure or pain, thrilled me because he brought it out.

I slid my fingers over my needy clit and rubbed, desperate for another release. Ryder plunged into me one final time and stilled as he came hard inside me, and seconds later, my orgasm raced through me and I joined him in our shared ecstasy.

He traced his finger down the center of my back and pressed a kiss on my spine. "I love the way your cunt feels when you come and I'm inside you," he whispered against my skin. "Still one of the best things in the world."

Leaning forward, I felt his cock slip out of me. I turned around and fell onto the bed, exhausted and unable to walk, just as he'd promised. Looking up at him as he sat back on his heels, I let my gaze glide over the muscular peaks and valleys of his beautiful body and the array of tattoos on his arms and chest and felt my desire to have him inside me rise again. Smiling proudly, he looked like some victorious hero.

"You always look very pleased with yourself after we're done, you know that? It's very sexy."

He crawled up my body and rested his head on the pillow next to me as his legs draped over mine. "I love watching you while I fuck you. You're so beautiful and so open for me, like your body was meant just for my cock."

I kissed him, loving how sexy I felt because of his words. "You were right. I can barely move my legs, much less walk."

Grinning, he leaned back. "Then my job is done here."

When he was cute like that, like when he and I spent time together in the spare bedroom right after he got to the estate, I couldn't help love him even more. We'd been so innocent back then. I'd been in love with him even before I had to leave for Italy, but still, things were so innocent.

He gave me something sweet I'd never had before, and I adored him for it.

Ryder touched my cheek and whispered, "Hey, where did you go there? You looked a million miles away."

I turned toward him and snuggled in the space between his neck and chin, nuzzling just under his ear. "I was just thinking about when we first met."

"It feels like forever ago, doesn't it?"

"It does. Promise me something, okay?"

He looked down at me and tilted my head back so we faced each other. "Anything. You know that."

I looked up into those green eyes so full of emotion and swore I'd never forget that. "Promise me no matter what happens for the rest of our lives, we'll remember how we were back then?"

A smile slowly spread across his mouth, and he softly kissed me on the forehead. "I never want to forget that time. That's where we started."

"I don't want to either. I never want to forget what made me fall in love with you."

"Bruises, tats, and muscles as I sat in the bathtub?" he joked.

I shook my head and kissed him on the cheek. "No. You made me feel loved and safe. I'd never felt like that before you came here."

Ryder pulled me to him and wrapped his arms around me. "You are loved, and I swear I will always protect you, Serena. Always."

From others, I may have doubted those words and feared they were meaningless and hollow. But not from Ryder. He'd proved time and again that he was the only person I could trust to keep me safe.

I may have found more strength than I ever thought I possessed now that Cayden was in my life, but we needed Ryder more than ever because my father still hadn't gotten his way.

And that was always a risk I knew all too well.

Chapter Six

Serena

"RYDER, I WANT my mother to see Cayden. It's been a month already since he came home. I've been as patient as I can be, but she's okay and I want her to meet her grandson."

He sighed and nodded, as if he'd resigned himself to me eventually asking for this. That didn't mean he liked the idea, though.

Looking back to make sure the nursery door was closed, he took a step closer to me and lowered his voice. "I know, but it's dangerous. Your father hasn't given up on finding her, Serena. He sent Jesse to kill her, and I don't believe for a second he doesn't still want that. Just because he's acting like grandfather of the year doesn't change who he is."

I knew all of this and still needed my mother to meet Cayden. I tried to find the words to explain to Ryder why this meant so much to me. "I'm sure you're right, but I need for her to know our son. I spent too many years with her gone from my life, and I don't want to repeat that with him."

"She's messaged twice," he said in a voice barely above a whisper. "I know where she is, but I'm not sure it's safe, Serena."

Cayden opened his mouth wide to yawn and closed his eyes, so I laid him down in his crib. After kissing him on the forehead, I turned back to Ryder, who stood watching him intently.

"I wish you could see the look on your face. That's what my mother is missing. I want her to have the chance to fall in love with him like we have. We can do this. I know we can. We just have to be safe."

Ryder lightly pressed his finger to my lips and looked up toward the ceiling. He scanned the room before returning his focus to me. "I'm not even sure it's safe to speak like this anywhere in this house. In the two weeks I've been working down in the security room, I've found more than a few strange things that make me think he might have parts of the estate bugged."

The uncertainty in his eyes worried me. I knew if he was worried that I had very good reason to be concerned too.

In his ear, I whispered, "There's got to be a way. She's his grandmother. I want her to see our son and get to spend time with him. I don't want to wait until we figure out where she's going to go and if we're going too."

Leaning away from him, I looked into his eyes

and hoped he understood why this meant so much to me. "Please don't say no to this."

"Give me a little time to figure out a way to make sure it's safe. I don't want to risk Robert having us tailed and finding out where she is."

I wrapped my arms around him and hugged him for giving me this. "Thank you! This means so much to me. Thank you for understanding."

✧ ✧ ✧

SITTING ON THE EDGE of our bed, I finished feeding Cayden and watched him babble in happiness at having a full belly. I looked down into his sleepy face as his eyelids fluttered closed and he lay there in my arms.

A noise outside in the hallway tore me from my reverie, and I looked up to see Ryder closing the door quickly behind him. The look on his face said something was wrong.

"If you want to go see her, now's the time. Your father and his guys are off to some meeting for a few hours."

I looked down at my son so content and asleep in my arms and then back at Ryder as I buttoned up my shirt. "Okay. Okay. Let me just get him ready. I didn't think it would be this soon. It's only been a day since I asked you about it."

"There isn't much time. I wrote down the

directions, so just use them and don't put anything into the GPS, just in case. You won't have more than a couple hours, so keep that in mind."

He handed me the piece of paper and took Cayden from me so I could put on a pair of shoes. I looked at him and wondered why he wasn't getting ready too.

"You aren't coming?"

Smiling down at the baby who had opened his eyes, he shook his head. "No, I can't risk it. It looks suspicious if we're both gone. This way it just looks like you took Cayden out to enjoy the nice weather."

"Okay. I'll have my phone with me if you need to call me or text me to let me know anything. Thank you. You have no idea how much this means to me. Is she expecting us?"

Ryder kissed the baby on the cheek and handed him to me. "Yeah. I talked to Michael about a half hour ago when I found out about your father's meeting. She can't wait to see you two."

I pressed a kiss onto Ryder's lips and wished he could come with us for this first meeting. "I love you. I'll see you in few hours, okay?"

He smiled and walked toward the bedroom door. Stopping just before he opened it, he turned toward me and said, "Don't take any pictures. I know you want to, but we have to be careful, Serena. Okay?"

Anger rose inside me, making me want to scream. "No pictures? I can't live like this for much longer, Ryder. Something has to give. I should be able to take pictures of Cayden and his grandmother together for the first time. It's never going to happen again."

Cradling my face in his palms, he nodded and I saw real sympathy in his eyes. "I know, but for now, this is how things are. We have to be careful or he might find her. We can't risk that. Now go and I'll see you in a few hours."

I knew he was right, but I hated living like this. I knew we had to stay there at the estate for a little while Ryder made enough money to send my mother someplace she could be safely hidden away and my father couldn't find her, but I didn't know how long I could stand being around him knowing what kind of person he really was.

At least my father had begun paying him for real and not just putting money into some account he could never touch. We had Cayden to thank for that since he seemed convinced babies required a great deal.

But more and more, I couldn't stand the idea of living in the same house as my father.

I DROVE THE CAR to the exit written on the piece of paper Ryder gave me and looked at the signs on the side of the road for Wisteria. Three other towns were listed above an arrow pointing left, but none by the name I saw written on the paper in my hand.

Turn right off the exit ramp and drive two miles, past an old barn with a sun painted on it, to Railroad Street in Wisteria. The house will be in the middle of the street. White house with blue shutters. Park on the street and go to the door at the back of the house.

Following his directions, I reached the house a few minutes later just as Cayden began fussing. Unlike other babies, car rides never seemed to lull him into a deep sleep. He was like me that way. I never liked long car rides either.

"It's okay, honey. We're here. Just wait. You get to meet your grandma today, so give me a few seconds to park the car and we'll go in."

He made a grunting noise that said my talking didn't make him any happier about being in his car seat for so long, and I quickly found a parking spot and got the two of us out of the car.

Just like when I walked up to that tiny carriage house a few months before, my heart pounded hard in my chest as I grew excited at seeing my mother again. This time, though, I had something even better than just myself for her.

This time I had her one and only grandchild for

her to meet for the very first time.

The door slowly opened and just like last time, my mother stared out in shock, her dark eyes wide as she looked at Cayden nestled in my arms. Waving us in, she reached out to take him and with a big smile said, "Oh, he's beautiful, Serena. Cayden, I'm your grandmother. It's so wonderful to meet you."

As if he knew exactly who she was, he turned his tiny mouth up into a smile, bringing tears to her eyes. I knew just how she felt. I'd been the same way the first time I saw him.

I closed the door behind us and followed her to the couch. "I'm so happy Ryder found a way for us to meet you, Mom. I've wanted you to see the baby all month."

She gazed at him like she'd never seen anything so wonderful in her life before finally looking up with tears in her eyes. "I always dreamed of this moment, you know that? I think I just naturally thought of it with a granddaughter, but this is even better than I ever imagined. He's perfect, honey."

"He is, isn't he? Sometimes after I feed him, I'll sit with him in my arms while he goes to sleep and all I do is stare at him and wonder how it's possible he could be so perfect."

My mother slid her finger into one of his palms, and Cayden instinctively wrapped his tiny fingers around hers. "He's strong. He gets that from his father, I bet," she said with a smile.

"I hope he's as strong as Ryder when he grows up."

"I owe Ryder my life, Serena. If it wasn't for him, both Michael and I would have been dead that night."

Hearing her praise him meant the world to me. "That's the kind of man he is, Mom. He's saved me so many times. And he's terrific with the baby too."

"Good," my mother said with a nod. "I want you to know I don't worry about you anymore because I know he's protecting you."

"He is. We have to stay where we are for the time being, but you don't have to worry about me. He wouldn't let anyone hurt me. Even Daddy."

My mother's expression grew dark at hearing we'd be staying at the estate for now. Frowning, she sighed and turned her attention back to Cayden. "I want both of you to be careful. I don't put anything past him anymore."

"I know," I admitted sadly, hating the truth about my father. "I knew he'd be angry we were talking, but I never imagined he'd send someone to kill you."

She looked up at me and shook her head. "Not just me, Serena. Michael too."

"Why would he want to kill his gardener?" I wondered, unless it was because my father knew he'd help her escape because he was a kind person.

My mother took a deep breath and let it out slowly as she tenderly stroked Cayden's cheek. "Michael wasn't just the gardener, Serena. He's my son and your brother."

Her words hit me like a bolt of lightning. My brother? I didn't have a brother. I knew my father well enough to know that if he had a son, that child would be by his side, not exiled to some house in the country. Whoever this Michael person was and whatever reason my mother called him her son, he wasn't my father's. That I knew for certain.

"How? When? It's always just been Janelle and me. We don't have a brother."

"You do, honey. Michael is my son with another man. After your father sent me to that house, I was sad and lonely. My life was over. I'd lost you two girls and I wasn't sure I could go on. But one of the men who worked on the grounds at the house there helped me see life was worth living, and we fell in love. Jonathan took care of me, and as things happen, I became pregnant."

My mouth hung open in shock. I had a brother. Quickly, my mind did the math. A brother seven years younger than me? I thought about meeting Michael that one time and how close to my age he looked. It all seemed to fit.

"Why didn't his father get you away from that

place all those years ago when he found out you were having his child?" I asked, my heart contracting at the very idea that my mother had been abandoned by not one but two men.

"Because he never had the chance. Your father had him killed when he found out, leaving me pregnant and alone. I was worried he might kill me then too or take the child away from me when I had a boy, but he simply left us out there."

She hadn't been abandoned. Once again, my father had punished her for simply trying to find a tiny sliver of happiness. Anger coursed through me at how many of us had suffered because of him.

"I'm so sorry, Mom. I can't believe how evil he is. So he just left you out there to raise a child on your own?"

Nodding, she sighed and looked down at Cayden. "Yes. I raised Michael on my own. Nobody knew he was there. He never went to school or anywhere off the estate. When he became a teenager, your father made him the gardener. It was his way of showing he possessed all the power, and he controlled us completely."

"Why didn't he take you away from there?"

"The little money your father paid him he spent to make sure I was taken care of, Serena. He stayed even when he became an adult and could have left to make a better life for himself in the world. I don't know where I'd be if it wasn't for Michael."

All of this made me hate my father even more. My mother, Janelle, Michael, Ryder, and I had all suffered because of my father's need to rule over us with an iron fist.

"Has he known about Janelle and me the whole time?"

Cayden began to cry, so I took him into my arms and gently patted his back as she told me about my brother. "I told him when he was a teenager that he had two sisters. I think at first he didn't understand how since it had been just the two of us for his entire life, but when he met you that day, he instantly felt a closeness with you. He hopes someday to meet Janelle too. He doesn't expect you to just start thinking of him as your brother, but I wish you'd give him a chance. For me."

"Of course! I don't hold anything against him, Mom. Is that why he isn't here now? He didn't have to stay away. I'd never want that for anyone just because of me."

My mother waved off my concerns. "No, he had to go out to get us some food for dinner later. He just figured I'd like the chance to meet my grandson for the first time if it was just the three of us. He'll be here next time. I hope there will be a next time because I want to be in Cayden's life, Serena."

"There will be," I reassured her as Ryder's

warnings repeated in my brain. "We just have to be careful. We can't let Daddy find out where you are. We can't trust that he won't try to kill you again."

That I had to even say those words still amazed me. My father had lied all those years about my mother's whereabouts, and then when I finally had the chance to reconnect with her, the monster had tried to kill her. He truly was the embodiment of evil.

We sat there silently as the truth of who my father was hung in the air between us. I wished I was like other children of wealthy families who had money at their disposal so I could just get all of us away from Robert Erickson's twisted world where he relished devising ways of punishing us for unknown and uncommitted crimes against him.

The baby made a little cooing noise that brought me out of my thoughts. Gently rubbing his belly, I couldn't help but smile. Even in the midst of all the madness my father forced on everyone around him, Cayden made life brighter just by being in it with us.

"How is your father with the baby, Serena?"

Just the question made me bristle. From the moment my father first saw my son, he had taken liberties with him that made me uneasy. The mere act of his holding Cayden before Ryder had the chance to seemed far too ominous for me.

His redesign of Janelle's room into a beautiful nursery had at first seemed like a generous gesture, but more and more it felt like my father had begun to transfer his obsession with Ryder to Cayden.

"I don't know, Mom. He hasn't done anything that from the outside would seem troublesome, but all the same, I'm worried. Ryder is too."

Her eyes filled with fear, even as she tried to keep her voice calm and measured. "As long as you haven't seen anything yet. I want you to keep your eyes open, though, okay? Make sure Ryder protects Cayden. If he was girl, I wouldn't be as worried, but because he's a boy..."

She didn't finish her sentence, but she didn't have to. I knew just what she meant. When my father looked at Cayden, it was as if he was looking at him as a king would an heir.

Like all his hopes and dreams for the future were invested in that one tiny soul.

I didn't want my father forcing his life on my son. I'd lived every day in his world, and I knew the ugliness it held. I'd seen what it had done to Ryder, and he was a grown man when he entered my father's world. Cayden was merely a baby, and I had a sinking feeling that my father had dreams of grooming him to be the next Robert Erickson.

He'd never had a son to give him a legacy, and for a time, he seemed to want to treat Ryder as that son. Now he appeared to be growing more and more obsessed with Cayden as that chance at a legacy.

But Ryder and I would never let that happen. We couldn't. We loved our son too much to let him become tainted by my father's evil. Whatever it took, we'd keep our little boy safe from all of that ugliness.

"Don't worry, Mom. We won't let Daddy hurt him."

She shook her head sadly. "It isn't hurting I'm worried about, sweetheart. It's exactly the opposite. One day it's a shiny new toy, and Cayden is thrilled, as he should be. The next time it's something more, something that makes him even more attached to your father. And all the while, he's molding him in exactly the way he wants him to think. Things are important. Money rules over all else. And people are disposable, pieces on his chessboard moved around at his will to further his and only his interests. I worried about it from the day you girls were born, but I think you were spared in some ways by not being boys. Cayden, like Ryder, doesn't have that benefit. Strangely enough, being male in your father's world might be worse than being female."

I couldn't imagine a fate worse than mine or Janelle's in this world. Traded to the highest bidders, we were viewed merely in what worth we could bring, not in what worth we possessed simply by being ourselves.

As much as I hated leaving my mother so soon, I knew I had to return to the estate so she wouldn't be in danger from someone finding me there. "I wish I could stay longer, Mom, but I have to go. I promise we'll see each other soon."

She looked up at me with disappointment but tried to smile through it. "I know. I've lived a lifetime like this. A little while longer isn't going to get me down. I'll just look forward to the next time I get to see you and my grandson."

"I promise we'll be back as soon as it's safe."

Kissing Cayden's fingers, she whispered against them, "I'm so happy to meet you, little Cayden. Come back and see your grandmother soon, okay?"

As I drove home, my mother's warning repeated in my mind. What she said rang true. I'd seen how my father had attempted to create a son out of Ryder. Now he had a grandson, his own flesh and blood he could pass on all he'd created to.

I didn't want my son being any part of those things. Whatever he was because of his family, he was Ryder's and my child before all else.

Chapter Seven

Serena

R YDER MET ME in Cayden's nursery as I began to feed him. Closing the door behind him, he walked over to where I sat in the rocking chair near the window and knelt down in front of me.

"Did everything go okay?" he asked in that concerned voice he seemed to use more and more lately.

I hated how worry seemed to forever be in his eyes these days. I wanted that intensity I loved to see in them return.

"It went great! It was so wonderful to see her and see the way she was with the baby. I knew she'd fall in love with him the moment she saw him."

He smiled and gently cupped the back of Cayden's head as he fed. "That's my son. Charming the ladies from day one."

"It really was wonderful, Ryder. She couldn't take her eyes off him, and he was such a good boy with her. He only cried a couple times on the way up and on the way back, but that's because he's the one baby in a million who doesn't like riding in a car."

"Good. I'm happy you two got to see her. I don't know when you'll get to again, but I'll keep my eyes open to see when Robert and his guys will be out for a few hours."

"Does he tell you his schedule? We might be able to find a way to let us see her sooner that way, and maybe you can come with us next time. I know she'd love to see you again."

His smile faded. Shaking his head, he said, "He doesn't let me know anything anymore. Not since he made me head of security here at the estate. I only know things when I overhear them or see him leave and his guys follow him out."

On the one hand, I liked that Ryder didn't take part in much of my father's day-to-day business now, but it would have made knowing when we could sneak away to see my mother much easier if he was still in the loop.

That I, a grown woman with a child, and my husband had to actually sneak anywhere at all showed how dysfunctional life in my father's world truly was. We couldn't change that, though, but we could do everything in our power to maneuver around it.

Ryder leaned forward to kiss the back of Cayden's head and then kissed me. "I have to get back now, but I have other news for you. Guess who's coming for a visit?" he said with a chuckle.

Quickly, I tried to think of anyone whose visit would amuse him like that, but I drew a blank. "I don't know. Who?"

"Janelle. Alone again. No Charles this time either."

Rolling my eyes, I let out a sigh of frustration. "Ugh. Another county heard from. Any idea why she's coming or for how long?"

He shrugged and sat back on his heels. "No idea. Robert just told me she'll be here tomorrow and to make sure she doesn't park her car in the garage. I'm like a parking attendant now."

I couldn't imagine why my father had given him those instructions, but the bigger issue still loomed. My sister, no matter how much she seemed to adore Cayden, would be a hassle and could cause a problem if we had the chance to sneak away to see my mother while she was around.

"See you later after work. Time for me to get back to Johnson and his fish tales. I'm beginning to think your father has finally come up with a real punishment for me, and it has nothing to do with beating me half to death. I think he plans to have Johnson bore me to death."

He stood up and smiled, and I loved seeing him like that. "Did you just make a joke?"

"I wish it was a joke. No, I think I might die

from boredom at this job, Serena."

Touching his hand, I squeezed it gently in mine. "I know you don't want to sit in front of those monitors and listen to fishing stories all day, but it means the world to me that you'd do it to help my mother, Ryder."

He leaned down and kissed me sweetly. "It's not so bad. I've done much worse things. I think I'm just worried because I'm not in the inner circle anymore. It makes me feel like we're vulnerable."

Cayden finished feeding, so I put him against my shoulder and gently rubbed his back to burp him as I tried to show his father how much I appreciated what he did for us every day. "Someday we're going to be far away from here, Ryder. Cayden and his brothers and sisters will never have to live with what we've been through here. I still believe that."

Pressing his forehead to mine, he smiled again. "Brothers and sisters? Is there something you forgot to tell me?"

I kissed the tip of his nose and giggled. "No. Not that I know of. But I don't want this little guy to be an only child."

"Okay. I have to get back to work, but I'm always ready to be on the job for the baby making." He kissed Cayden on the top of his head and whispered, "See you later, buddy. Be good for your mother."

I watched him walk away and longed for that

day when he didn't have to work as the head of security and our family lived far away from this place.

✦ ✦ ✦

JANELLE MADE A BEELINE down the hall toward me as I closed the door to the bedroom. Arms open, she squealed, "Where is that nephew of mine? I need to see that adorable little face again! It's been too long since I had my dose of Vitamin C."

To see her practically giddy to see anyone but the person in the mirror made me suspicious. I didn't know who this person was or what she'd done with my sister, but I knew there was no way the old Janelle would act this way.

"He's still down for a nap, but he'll be up in a little while when it's time for his lunch," I said, stepping in front of her as she turned toward her old room. "Where are you staying while you're here? In one of the apartments?"

She shook her head but looked confused by my directing her away from Cayden's nursery. "No. I…I'm staying in the guest room. You know, the one where Ryder stayed in when he first came here."

I physically moved her down the hall toward the staircase. "Why don't we go down there while Cayden sleeps then?"

"What if he wakes up? Shouldn't we hang out

nearby?"

I dangled the baby monitor in front of me. "Got it covered. If he makes a peep, I'll know about it. So we can relax and catch up until then."

In truth, I didn't really know what Janelle and I would talk about, even if Cayden only slept for another five minutes. We'd never been close, especially since I didn't trust her as far as I could throw her, so sisterly talks had never really been a thing for us.

She seemed different lately, though, so maybe we could find some topic of conversation to fill the minutes before the baby woke up for his feeding. As long as we kept to things like her life, her house, and her vacation plans, I didn't believe it would be too risky to spend time with her.

Boring, but not risky.

"Okay, but I want to spend some time with him while I'm here. Maybe I could babysit so you and Ryder can go out. Since you won't use a nanny, I'm sure you guys haven't had much chance to go out on a date or anything."

I opened my mouth to say now that we're married it wouldn't exactly be a date, but I stopped myself. Janelle couldn't be trusted, and I didn't want my father to know we'd gotten married yet.

We headed toward the guest room as I thought about leaving Cayden alone with my sister. The mere thought terrified me. She might get bored with him and forget all about feeding or changing him. Or worse, she might let my father do something with him.

"Well, maybe. I'm still recuperating from giving birth, so I'm pretty tired most nights," I lied, barely able to keep a straight face as I said those words. I'd been in labor for a grand total of five hours, and the actual birth had gone more smoothly than any the doctor had experienced before.

She stopped at the bedroom door and nodded like she fully understood what I'd been through and truly sympathized. "I'm totally in awe of what you went through, Serena. I don't know if I could be that strong."

The desire to roll my eyes nearly overwhelmed me, but thankfully, Janelle turned away to walk into her temporary room. I followed her in and stopped just inside the door, struck by the memories that place held for me.

I'd gotten to know the man I loved in that room. We'd talked about so much all those nights. In those first months, he'd become a lifeline for me, giving me hope I'd never known before.

Looking over toward the bed, I remembered lying there every night with my head on his shoulder and falling asleep feeling safe for the first time in my life. As I stared at the grey bedspread, I couldn't help but miss those times together. We were so innocent then. So hopeful.

I wanted to believe we could still hope for that future. We'd overcome all the obstacles to being together and even begun our own family. But we still remained trapped in my father's world for now, even though I had to believe that wouldn't last forever.

Janelle extended her arm and gestured toward the bed. "Sit down. We'll talk until that adorable baby of yours wakes up."

Something in her tone sounded off, which immediately set me on edge. Had my father brought her here to help him do something to Ryder or me or both of us?

"Okay. What do you want to talk about?" I asked, afraid to hear her answer.

She sat down across from me and frowned. "I don't know. Anything, I guess."

"Is everything okay, Janelle? You look sad."

Nodding, she forced a smile. "Yeah. Everything's fine."

She didn't look fine, and she certainly didn't sound fine. "If you want to talk about something, I'm here."

"It's nothing."

"Is everything okay with Charles? We haven't seen him in a while."

She shrugged and the frown returned. "I guess. I

wouldn't really know, to be honest."

"Because he's always working?" I asked, sensing his job wasn't the problem between them.

Looking away from me, she said, "No. Because we haven't lived together for the last three months."

"What? Why?" I sat there stunned by her admission.

Slowly, she turned back toward me with tears in her eyes. "He's with another woman. She's someone he works with. I guess they fell in love on the job. Like that's okay."

"Oh, Janelle. I'm so sorry. I had no idea."

Everything I'd always feared would happen to her because she had let herself be dependent first on my father and then Charles had come true, but I didn't enjoy hearing my sister tell me her marriage lay in ruins. If anything, it made me feel pity for her, not want to gloat that I'd been right all along.

"I guess I should have listened to you when you said marrying Charles was a mistake," she said, hanging her head.

"I didn't mean he was bad. I just didn't think you should have to marry someone because Daddy wanted you to. That was all. I truly hoped it would turn out good, though."

"Well, it didn't, and I have no one but myself to blame." She looked up at me and continued, "You have the right idea, you know that? Be with a man and even have babies with him, but never marry him."

The way she characterized my relationship with Ryder bothered me, but I couldn't admit the truth about how we'd already gotten married in secret. I didn't think the words would be out of my mouth for five minutes before she ran down the hall and told my father.

So I pushed down my desire to defend what we had together and simply smiled. "We're different people from you and Charles. It just works for us."

"Is that why you two haven't married yet, even though you have Cayden?" she asked, suddenly more interested in my romantic life than her own misery.

"What do you mean?"

"Is it that you don't love Ryder? That is your litmus test for marriage, isn't it? You thought it was wrong for me to marry Charles because I didn't love him. So is that why you and Ryder aren't married yet?"

Her questions caught me off guard, and I leaned back away from her, needing room to breathe. "Of course I love him. He's been the one person in my life who I could count on no matter what. He saved me when I tried to kill myself, and then he saved me from Oliver. I love Ryder more than I can even explain."

"Then why not marry him?" she asked, pressing

the issue.

As she waited with bated breath for my answer, I tried to come up with one she'd accept so she'd drop the subject entirely. Since we didn't see anything, including love, in the same way, it might be impossible.

Finally, I simply said, "Maybe I will. That's if Daddy doesn't stop us, of course."

She rolled her eyes and waved away my concern. "Are you kidding? He's crazy about Ryder. I think he might fall over and die from joy if you told him you and Ryder were getting married."

I stared at her wondering if Janelle had simply been away so long that she didn't know all that had happened and my father hadn't told her or if she knew full well about the bad feelings between them and was baiting me to say something.

Either way, I didn't want to talk to her about this anymore.

"Have you told Daddy about Charles and you?" I asked, eager to change the topic.

"No. Why would I? You know how he hates to be disappointed."

And that in a nutshell explained the differences between my sister and me. She still cared that her news would upset him. Even after he married her off to a man based on how much he made and how he could help him instead of her, she still worried about disappointing him.

Those days were long gone for me. Now I kept things hidden from my father for strategic reasons. I didn't care about how anything I did made him feel. I was a grown woman, a mother of a newborn and the wife of a man I loved. The only people in the world I worried about disappointing was them.

"Well, he'll just have to deal with it when it all comes out," I said, completely disinterested in the idea of making my father's life easier. "He'll just have to understand."

Janelle bit her lip nervously for a few moments and then said, "You know, I was thinking the other day that I wish I could talk to Mom. Maybe she'd know what I should do because some days I don't feel like I'm handing this whole Charles thing well. I thought I could because he's still supporting me and I thought that would make me accept things, but some days it just feels like I want to scream at the top of my lungs that the money isn't enough. That he said the same vows as I did, and even if we didn't mean them a hundred percent, we still were supposed to act like we did."

Excitement grew inside me at the mere thought of Janelle finally joining me when I next visited my mother. I wanted to tell her just talking to her would make her see things in a totally new way. I wanted to share how wonderful our mother was with her.

But I didn't.

I curbed my enthusiasm and bit my tongue because the truth was I couldn't trust Janelle. As much as I wished I could, I couldn't risk my mother's safety by telling my sister she was still alive and wanted to talk to her too.

A noise from the baby monitor interrupted us, and Janelle excitedly pointed at it. "Does that mean he's awake and ready to see his Auntie Janelle?"

"Yep. We can go see him now."

My sister jumped up from the bed and was out the door into the hallway before my feet hit the floor. For all the horrible things I'd thought about her through the years, she certainly seemed to love my son.

For that, I had to admit I liked her a little more these days.

✧　✧　✧

RYDER SLID HIS ARM around me and kissed my neck. "So how bad was it with your sister today?"

I rolled over to face him and looked into his eyes as what she said about us replayed in my mind. "I love you. You know that, right?"

A look of confusion came over him. Nodding, he said, "Of course. Did Janelle say something about us that made you upset? Is that where this is coming from?"

Cradling his face, I stopped his talking with a kiss. "No. I just don't want you to ever think I don't love you more than I can even say."

"Okay. I don't think that, though. What's going on, Serena?"

I hesitated to say anything about what Janelle and I talked about, but finally I said, "My sister asked me if the reason we aren't married is because I don't love you. It bothers me that she might think that because she doesn't know we already got married."

My confession made him smile. "I thought we agreed to keep things quiet for now. I don't care what the rest of the world thinks. I care what you think. I know you love me, Serena, just like you know I love you."

He kissed me and pulled me close to him, and I knew he was right. It didn't matter what anyone thought we had together. All that mattered was we knew how we felt about one another.

"I do know you love me, Ryder. I've never doubted it for a single moment."

"Good. So about that baby making? I think tonight we might give Cayden a little brother or sister."

When he said things like that, I couldn't help but love how cute he could be. "You think?"

He smiled a devilish grin as he slid his hand between my legs and stroked my tender skin. "I don't think it could hurt to try."

Closing my eyes, I pushed away everything from the day—my time with Janelle, thinking about my father, and even being Cayden's mommy—and just let myself enjoy being with the man I loved. Ryder kissed his way down over my ribs as his fingers slid inside me, making my body come alive.

"Ohhh, that feels so good. I love when you do that."

He looked up as he kissed across my belly and smiled. "This is just the prelims. Babies don't get made this way."

I pulled him on top of me and kissed him hard on the mouth. "I know how they get made, sir. This isn't my first rodeo, you know."

Staring down at me, he smiled. "Rodeo? I like the sound of that. Maybe we can do the bucking bronco."

"What is that? On second thought, don't tell me. I don't think I want to know."

I opened my legs and wrapped them around his waist, urging him inside me. The tip of his cock nudged me open, and in seconds, he was buried inside me, completely filling me.

"No bucking bronco tonight then," he said as he began to slide in and out of me. "Another time maybe. For now, I'm liking the idea of just making love to my wife."

Moaning with each time his cock hit that place

inside that felt so fucking good, I thought to myself that I liked that idea too. I didn't need anything more than Ryder's love. I never had.

Tonight was about the love we shared, and as we slowly inched each other toward that delicious edge, we joined together maybe to make a child or maybe to simply enjoy one another. Whatever happened, we'd get through what the future held for us.

We always had because of our love.

Chapter Eight

Ryder

A STREAM OF CARS raced by as I searched for a parking space in front of the medical arts building where Cayden had his three month checkup. Serena clutched the baby's diaper bag and impatiently tapped her foot with each moment that passed and I still hadn't parked the car.

"Ryder, we're almost late. We need to get in there."

Cayden chimed in with his own complaining and began to cry, completing the dissatisfaction of the two people I cared about in this world.

I shifted the car into park and turned to look at Serena. "I'll drop you off and find a spot."

"You're coming in, right? I want you to be there with us."

Serena had been worried for days, and I'd tried to convince her everything about Cayden was perfect, but each time he fed, she became more stressed that something was wrong with him. Thankfully, his checkup was today, so I hoped the doctor would help her see what I saw—that our son was a normal and happy baby boy.

"It's okay. You don't have to be worried. Cayden's a healthy kid."

She began to protest but then stopped and blew the air out of her lungs. "I just want the doctor to see he's doing fine, but he doesn't seem to be growing like all the books say he should be. And lately, he doesn't want to eat as much. I think he doesn't want breastmilk anymore."

I kissed her and pushed her hair behind her ear. "It's going to be okay. Don't worry, all right?"

With a heavy sigh, she nodded and forced a smile. "Okay. We better get inside or we're really going to be late."

Looking out at the side mirror, I saw a line of cars coming toward us. "Just give me a second and I'll get out and get the baby."

"No, you'll get run over, Ryder. I'll get him, and you come up as soon as you find a spot, okay?"

I smiled at her, loving how thoughtful she was. "Give me five minutes and I'll be there with bells on."

She leaned over and kissed me quickly before jumping out of the car. In seconds, she had Cayden and his carrier out, and I watched as she lugged it and the diaper bag up the sidewalk before she disappeared into the building.

Everybody in the world seemed to be in this part of Baltimore at the same time we had to be, so I finally gave up searching for a space and parked the car in a parking garage. I'd have to walk three blocks to get back to the doctor's office, but if I hurried, I might not miss the whole appointment.

I headed toward the elevator and pressed the button to go down to the ground floor just as two men in dark suits walked up to stand behind me. Eager to get to the doctor's office, I pressed the button again and heard one of the men say, "Mr. Rhodes, we'd like to talk to you. Do you have a moment?"

My blood ran cold at the sound of the stranger saying my name. Slowly, I turned around and looked at both men. They didn't look like the kind of guys Robert kept around him. They had a stiffness and a classiness Robert's men lacked. Neither one looked big enough that I couldn't take him, but two was a different story.

More importantly, if they weren't Robert's men, who were they and how did they know my name?

"You must have me mistaken for someone else," I said, turning back to face the elevator doors. Not that the elevator coming would give me any real escape since I had a feeling they planned to ride down with me.

"No mistake, Mr. Rhodes."

Staring straight ahead, I didn't answer. For a moment, there was silence behind me, but then the man began speaking again. "Prostitution, gambling, illegal underground fighting—these are all part of the world your son will grow up in. Is that what you want? You've seen that life firsthand, Mr. Rhodes. Do you want that for your son? For your wife?"

His words stopped my breathing for a moment. I never wanted that for Serena or Cayden. Both were more precious to me than my own life, and I spent every waking moment thinking of how I could protect them from all of that ugliness. I wanted to believe that maybe my son would grow up untouched by it all like his mother had, but I knew better. I'd wanted to get Serena away from that world the minute I realized what it was.

Staring straight ahead at the black elevator doors, I answered him. "I'm sorry. I don't know what you're talking about."

The two men stepped around me so I couldn't avoid facing them any longer. They looked at me with steely eyes that said they knew everything. I didn't have to guess who they were anymore.

"We'd like to talk to you about your son's grandfather. We think you know what we mean. The FBI knows all about what's been going on."

I nodded, but I couldn't help them. I wasn't going to be the one who'd turn Robert over to the authorities.

They waited for me to say something, and when I didn't, the man on the right reached into his suit coat and pulled out a card. Handing it to me, he said, "When you're ready to talk. But know this. Right now, you're part of his world and as guilty as he is. You're not who we want, though."

I looked at the card and then back up at him, meeting his hard gaze with mine. "I can't help you."

His mouth stretched into a tight smile. "Keep it for when you can. But don't wait too long."

The two men walked away just as the elevator doors opened, and by the time I stepped in and turned around to look out, they were gone from sight. Alone in the elevator, I watched as the doors closed and the car jolted on its down to the ground floor.

I tried to imagine a world without Robert in control. A world where Serena and I could leave the estate with Cayden and go anywhere we wanted to. We could go to that little house she dreamed of with the white picket fence and a yard for our son to play in. Or we could go to that place in the mountains where we could be alone and never have to deal with the demands of others again.

We'd wished for those things for so long. Now it seemed like that chance had finally come, but could I do that to the man who'd called me his son?

I knew what he meant when he said I was his adopted son. Every time the words left his mouth, they were his not-so-subtle way of forcing Serena and her sister to understand how little he thought of them because they had the misfortune of being born the wrong sex.

The bad luck of being born female.

But I, some stray he found hiding away in his warehouse, was given the title of son, even though I didn't deserve the respect that came from the name. The respect that rightfully belonged to his daughters but had never been given because they weren't male.

I knew all this and still couldn't imagine being the one to deliver the final blow that would end him. Even though doing so would free Serena and Cayden from him, I still couldn't fathom doing that.

What the fuck was wrong with me? I should have jumped at the chance to rid my life of Robert Erickson. He'd tormented the woman I loved and had me beaten senseless. He'd done everything in his power to keep Serena and me apart. And I suspected at some point he'd order my death as he'd ordered so many others.

And yet still I couldn't bring myself to do what it took to take him down.

I tried to remember all the bad I'd experienced since meeting him, but every time I did, all that flooded my brain were thoughts of all those times he didn't send me away when I betrayed him. Sure, he'd made sure I fought an opponent I had no chance of beating, and he'd had me beaten senseless for what I'd done to Oliver.

But when I needed him most to let me be there for Serena and our son, Robert moved every legal mountain and even agreed to support that fighter for the rest of his life after the mistake I made while I was fighting behind his back. He could have made sure I went away—away from Serena, away from his life, away forever—never seeing my child.

He didn't do that to me. It was because of Robert that I got to stand over Cayden's crib and watch him sleep so peacefully at night. It was because of what he did that I had the chance to be with the woman I love.

How could I turn around and hand him over to the Feds? He'd done terrible things, but still all that stood out in my mind was the good.

I sat down on a bench outside the doctor's office and wondered if I was losing my mind. Those two had handed me a get out of jail free card. All I had to do was use it. So why couldn't I even bring myself to think about doing that?

My mind went back to one night a few months after Serena left and I came back to work for him when he turned to me as I stood in my usual place near the bookcase. His eyes narrowed and he stared at me like I'd said something that had angered him. I waited for him to bark at me about whatever he thought I'd done, but he simply stared for a few moments longer before he closed his laptop and walked over to the bar to make his usual bourbon and branch.

When he finished dropping the ice cubes into his glass, he looked over at me and I felt his intense gaze on me like a laser burning into my cheek. I turned to face him, expecting some reprimand, but still he said nothing.

Only after he'd downed half a glass of his drink did he finally speak. In a low voice, he asked, "Do you think I would know if one of my men was speaking to the Feds, Ryder?"

He rarely talked about the police at all. The local cops enjoyed being in his pocket, mostly because they got preferential treatment at the strip clubs and with the girls, and even the Baltimore cops seemed willing to look the other way when it came to the fights. So to hear him ask about one of us talking to the authorities felt off, like he was testing me.

"I think you know everything that happens with every one of us, Robert."

I'd only been working as his security for a few months then, so I hadn't realized by that time that while he knew a lot about what went on with his employees, he didn't know everything. Then I still believed in him as some all-knowing type of boss.

"You think so, son? You think anyone would be stupid enough to cross me like that?" he asked sharply, making me wonder if I'd given the wrong answer.

Hoping to soothe his anger, I nodded. "I do. We know better than to fuck with you, Robert. You're not the type of man to let disloyalty go unpunished, and for opening our mouths when we shouldn't, you'd kill us."

He laughed at my answer and walked back to his desk, chucking me on the shoulder as he passed me. "I like the way you think of me, Ryder. I just wonder if the rest of my employees think that way."

My mind raced with thoughts of who he could be talking about. Had one of us gone to the authorities? Why would any of us talk to them? Each person I thought of I dismissed out of hand. None of us were that stupid.

"I'm sure they do, Robert. Loyalty is something expected. We all know that."

He nodded, smiling like he liked my answer. After taking another sip of his drink, he set the glass down on his desk. "I think I would know if any one of my employees was betraying me to the FBI, and as soon as I found out about it, I'd do the only thing I could to protect myself. I'd kill them."

Hearing Robert threaten to kill someone had

become a daily occurrence once I began working for him as one of his men, but it never ceased to bother me how effortlessly that threat came out of his mouth.

I didn't know if I was expected to say something after that, but saying he'd kill anyone who dared to be disloyal made me unsure what my next sentence should be. He didn't seem interested in continuing the conversation, though, and returned to working on his laptop, leaving me alone with my thoughts about what the hell all of that had been about.

Robert had always been so careful in the past, but now as I sat outside Cayden's doctor's office, I wondered if things had changed in the months I'd been sitting in that security room with Johnson. Had Robert gotten sloppy in that time and given the FBI a way inside his organization?

No matter how much I might want to know, I couldn't be the one who turned on him. Not after what he did to save me from going to jail. He was the only reason I got to hold my son every day and sleep in the same bed next to Serena at night. I wouldn't stand in the way of someone else betraying him to the FBI, but it wouldn't be me.

I stood to head into the doctor's office to join Serena and the baby but saw her carrying him, the carrier, and the diaper bag out through the glass front doors. Rushing toward her to help, I grabbed the bag and the car seat as she held onto Cayden.

"What happened to you? I thought you were going to come in for the appointment?" she asked as she sat down on the bench I'd just left. Her tone and knitted brows told me she was none too happy I hadn't done as I said I would.

"It took me a while to find a parking spot. I had to go to a garage a few blocks away, and by the time I got back, I figured I missed the whole thing anyway." I bent down to kiss her and then Cayden. "What did the doctor say about our little guy? He's perfectly healthy, right?"

"You looked like you were a million miles away sitting here basking in the sun. Next time, you get to take the baby and all his stuff into his appointment," she said, pouting.

"Don't be mad at me. I was just thinking about how much I love my wife and son."

Serena rolled her eyes and laughed. "Nice try, pal."

I took a seat next to her and kissed her on the cheek. "Well, I was. So tell me all about what the doctor said about our son."

For a moment, she hesitated, like she couldn't decide whether to stay angry at me or not, but she chose to tell me what had happened in the appointment. "He's in the ninetieth percentile for his height and the eightieth percentile for his weight.

Doctor Sanders says he's growing just like he should be, and if I want to continue breastfeeding, I should. But he told me if I can't or Cayden doesn't want to anymore, it's not a sin to use formula."

I smiled, happy that both the people I loved more than life itself were doing just fine. "See? I knew everything would be okay. Both mommy and baby are perfect."

"I'm still a little angry that you didn't come in to the appointment, Ryder."

"How about I make it up to you by taking us all out to lunch?" I asked as I took Cayden out of her arms.

"You don't have to get back to work immediately?"

"No. I work for our son's grandfather. If he asks where I was, I'll just tell him I had to take you and Cayden to his doctor's appointment."

Her eyebrows shot up into her forehead. "So you'll lie?"

"No lie. I drove you here. I never said I'd tell him I went in with you two," I said with a chuckle.

Serena smirked. "Funny."

Holding Cayden up in front of me, I pressed my forehead to his. "What do you say we take your mom to lunch to celebrate, little man?"

He gurgled, which I took to mean he liked the idea, and Serena asked, "What are we celebrating?"

I leaned over and kissed her. "The perfect life with the perfect woman and our perfect son."

She didn't ask for a real answer, and I was happy she didn't. I liked being away from the estate, just the three of us enjoying our time together. Returning to the house meant going back to that life, and for just a few hours, I wanted us to live like normal people.

I didn't want to think about how normal people didn't usually get approached by the FBI about turning on their son's grandfather, a man who had committed enough crimes to be put away for the rest of his time on earth. I just wanted to enjoy a sunny day with my wife and son.

That wasn't too much to ask, was it?

Chapter Nine

Serena

LIVING A LIE was a never-ending series of worries and fears, but I had to keep up appearances to live the life I wanted. At least for the time being. To my father, I looked like the perfectly happy and content mother of a baby boy and girlfriend of a man she loved. I smiled whenever I saw him, even as I wanted to scream at the top of my lungs what kind of monster he truly was.

There would come a time when I would open my mouth and tell the world what life with him had been like, but not now. Now I'd continue to pretend because I knew if he learned where my mother was hiding, he'd hurt her.

Or worse.

So I waited. I'd spent my entire life looking to a future when I'd be happy, so this was no different, except now I had the man of my dreams and a baby I adored. True, we had to live on the estate, but that wouldn't last forever. We had all we needed. Now we just had to wait for that one final piece to complete the puzzle.

The time was coming when everything would change. I felt it. Someday soon, my father wouldn't have the power he lorded over us anymore. And when that day came, Ryder and I would leave this place with our son and never look back.

By the time Cayden was four months old, I saw my mother at least once a week and talked to her on the phone when I couldn't sneak out to go to her house. I even considered taking Janelle with me someday soon. I didn't feel ready to just yet, but I saw signs in her now that she'd lived through a bad marriage forced on her by my father that said she was changing too.

I dressed Cayden in a pair of blue shorts and a red t-shirt that said Daddy's Little Devil to go visit my mother and carried him downstairs to get him settled in his car seat. Since he didn't enjoy riding in the car, getting him comfortable so he wouldn't get an upset stomach took a while.

Passing my father's office on my way out, I didn't look in to say goodbye, preferring to stay away from him when I had the baby with me.

"Where are you going, Serena?" he yelled out as I grabbed the doorknob on the front door to leave.

"Just out for a little while," I answered, eager to get away before he wanted to have some long-winded conversation about something I didn't want to talk about, or worse yet, hold the baby and keep us there.

"Come in here," he said in a sharp tone that told me it wasn't a request.

My chest tightened and my stomach instantly twisted into a tight knot. I'd tried to avoid my father as much as possible in the months since we'd brought Cayden home from the hospital. I intentionally spent most of my time hidden away in the nursery so I could make sure he didn't see him. I didn't know why just having him hold my son bothered me so much, but it did and now as I slowly walked toward his office, I wanted nothing more than to run away with Cayden and never come back.

"We were just on our way out," I explained as I stood outside in the hallway looking into his office.

"Come in here and let me see my grandson," he said, waving me into the room.

Two large men stood in front of the bookcases and another stood just inside the door practically blocking the entrance. I didn't want to take a baby into that room. The mere idea terrified me.

"I think it might be better if Cayden wasn't around your work, Dad," I said quietly, pressing my cheek to the top of the baby's head.

He looked confused for a moment and then ordered the three men out of the room. Stepping away from the door, I watched as they dutifully filed out past me into the hallway. None of them gave either me or the baby the briefest look, thankfully, but they still made me feel uneasy.

My father stood from behind his desk and walked over to where I stood, stopping so close next to me that his body touched my arm as I held Cayden. "Now come in. Let me see that grandson of mine. How is it I live in the same place as he does but I never see him?"

Before I could say no, he reached down and took my son from me, as easily as a vulture swooping down to snatch up its prey. I stood there in shock as he walked away from me, turning his back so I couldn't even see the baby anymore.

"Dad, what did you want? I'm sure you're very busy with work and everything, so if you can just hand Cayden back to me, we'll leave you alone and not bother you," I said as I followed him into his office.

He looked back at me and grimaced. "You're not bothering me in the least, Serena. Why would you think I wouldn't want to take time out of my day to see my grandson?"

I didn't have an answer to his question. All I knew was every second I stood there watching him hold the baby, I felt like my world was spinning out of control. My emotions began to whirl inside me as fear and anxiety built higher and higher.

"We were just leaving to go out for a while," I explained, desperately hoping he'd give Cayden back to me.

"Were you going out?" he asked Cayden as he took him to sit on his lap in his office chair. "Is today a day out for the little boy?"

I hated the cutesy sound of his voice when he spoke to the baby. I never wanted my son to believe that tone meant he could be sweet or kind. He couldn't. Or wouldn't. Whichever it was, I cringed as he continued to pretend to be some doting grandparent.

My father placed Cayden's chubby hand on the top of his laptop and pushed down to close it. Turning his body so he faced him on his lap, he smiled down at him in a way a stranger might think was adorable.

I knew better.

"So now the bad work is put away, and I can spend time with my grandson. Right, Cayden?" he said, fawning over him as my stomach turned.

"Dad, we really need to go," I said in a voice that came out as pleading.

Without even looking at me, he pointed his finger toward one of the chairs in front of his desk. "Sit down, Serena. I'm enjoying time with my grandson. Let me have this, at least."

Tears welled in my eyes as I felt my control

quickly slipping away. I'd had nightmares about this from the day Cayden was born. When my father wanted something, he simply took it, and he'd taken my son.

No asking. Just taking.

My hands began to shake as I tightly clutched the baby bag and watched my father as he bounced Cayden on his lap. He didn't smile because he didn't like to be bounced. He hated moving like that. He wasn't like other babies. Car rides made him cry.

Don't do that.

Don't do that.

Stop bouncing him like that!

I reached over his desk toward him. "Dad, Cayden doesn't like bouncing like that. Please don't do that. It makes him upset."

He didn't stop moving his knee up and down but turned toward me with a look of disgust on his face. "Serena, what the hell is wrong with you? Most mothers would give their eye teeth for a few moments of rest from a newborn. Take advantage of the fact that my grandson and I get along and enjoy it."

I couldn't enjoy it. I could barely stand it. Just the sight of him holding my son terrified me. I didn't want Cayden to get along with my father. The man was a monster. My father was the type of person Ryder and I would do anything to protect our son from.

"He just doesn't like bouncing, Dad. Please don't make him sick."

My second request made him stop. "Fine. No more bouncing. You know, Serena, you can't hover over boys like you are. You're going to make him a sissy. Boys need room to be boys. Ask Ryder. He'll tell you."

"I'm not hovering. I'm his mother, and because I pay attention to him, I know he doesn't like to be bounced around. Some kids like that, but mine doesn't. Ask his father. He knows."

My response made my father's eyebrows rise in surprise, like he hadn't expected me to have anything to say to his edict on how I should be raising my own child. Whatever he thought, I didn't plan on just sitting by and letting my son be made sick simply because his grandfather had a penchant for bouncing children around.

"As for his father, how is our Ryder doing? I haven't had time to check on him down in that room with Johnson. Is he happy doing that now?"

Our Ryder. The way he referred to him never failed to make me cringe. He wasn't our anything. He was my Ryder. My husband. Mine. Not his.

"Ryder is fine. He's quite happy working as head of security here so he can spend time with me and Cayden."

"Why isn't he taking you wherever you and Cayden are going?" he asked as he began to bounce the baby on his knee again.

I glared at him and answered, "He's working, Dad. And I can go out with the baby just fine. Would you please stop bouncing him?"

Completely disregarding the frantic tone in my voice as I asked that question, he continued and said, "I don't want you out without someone guarding you and my grandson."

Cayden's pudgy little face twisted into the unhappy look he always wore right before he began to cry, so I quickly stood and walked around the desk to take him from my father. Just as the tears began to flow, I picked him up and cradled him in my arms.

"We don't need a guard, Dad. We have Ryder," I said as I stepped back away from behind the desk.

My father stared up at me with a look of surprise like he couldn't believe I would ever take the child back from him. "Well, he's busy now, so I want one of my other men to be with you to make sure you're safe."

Horrified at his suggestion that I knew would keep me from seeing my mother, I shook my head. "Safe from what? We're just going out for a drive. I don't need one of your men for that."

That familiar and horrible crocodile smile

spread across my father's face, stopping me as I took another step back toward the door. "You just said he doesn't like to be bounced. Why would you be going for a drive?"

"I figured out a way to make him comfortable. We're going out because it's nice to leave the house every so often, Dad. We don't need protection to take a short drive."

But he refused to relent. "I won't let anything happen to you or my grandson, Serena."

My emotions began to spiral out of control again as I saw my chance to visit with my mother slipping away right before my eyes. "Nothing is going to happen. I won't be watched like a child! I won't have one of your men following me around watching my every move!"

Cayden began to cry from my yelling, so I quickly pulled him to me and held him close. I knew coming in here would be a bad idea.

"I have to go, Dad."

Instead of saying anything in response to my obvious desire not to be watched over by one of his goons, he picked up the phone and began speaking to someone. Taking my opportunity to leave, I turned around to find the door blocked by one of the men who'd been standing in front of the bookcase.

"What is this?" I asked as I turned around to face my father. "Are you going to have him block my way out?"

"I won't be disobeyed on this point, Serena. If you're leaving this house, one of my men is going with you. Period."

My mind raced to find a way around this new rule he'd imposed. "So even if Ryder is with us, we have to have one of your men come too?"

He shook his head and waved away my suggestion. "Of course not. I trust Ryder more than anyone else to protect you and my grandson."

"Fine. Then I'll wait until he's finished with work and we'll go then."

Turning on my heels, I took a step to leave and saw the ignorant giant still blocking the doorway. "Would you move? My son and I need to leave. Now."

He looked right over my head toward my father for the answer to whether he should move out of the way or not. I didn't look back as tears of frustration began to well in my eyes again, and a second later, the man stepped out of the way.

Over my dead body would I have one of those damn thugs around my son every time we left the house. I'd just have to find another way to get to see my mother.

Can't go today. Come up to the room when you can. Need to talk.

I sent off my text to Ryder and called my mother as I paced back and forth across the carpeting in the bedroom. She answered the phone and without even saying hello, I began to talk, my utter frustration flowing out of my mouth.

"He insists that I have one of his goons with me whenever I leave the house. I'm not going to let him do this to me, though. I will find a way to get to see you, Mom. His ridiculous rules aren't going to stop me any longer."

My mother listened to me rant about my father, and when I finished, she asked the question that had run through my mind more than once since my father pulled me into his office that morning.

"Do you think he knows you've been coming to see me?"

I stopped walking and sat down on the bed next to Cayden as he slept like nothing was wrong in the world. Sliding my index finger into his hand, I watched him grip it with his chubby little fingers and tried to calm down.

"I don't know. I don't think so. Ryder has been very careful, Mom. We only come to see you when everyone is gone out, and we always come back before they do."

"Oh, honey, I don't doubt that Ryder is being as careful as he can be. This all just seems very sudden. It makes me wonder if your father knows something."

As Cayden squeezed my finger, I closed my eyes and tried to remember anything my father said that might tell us what he was up to. Nothing stuck out as an obvious clue as to why he suddenly felt the need for me to have a shadow whenever I left the estate.

"He didn't say anything that made me think he knows, Mom. I don't know. I'm tired of wondering if he's been spying on me or if he knows something I don't want him to know. I'm just so tired."

I didn't mean to make it sound like I had it harder than she did. For God's sake, my mother was forced to hide out in a tiny two bedroom house in a strange town she'd never heard of before a few months ago. For all the awful things we had to deal with, she was suffering far more than either Ryder or me.

But something about having to stand up to my father today just wiped me out. All I wanted to do was close my eyes and fall asleep with the hope that when I woke up, the nightmare of living in my father's world would be over.

"Honey, don't worry. I'll miss seeing you and Cayden today, but we'll see each other soon. Just be careful, okay? And take it easy on yourself. You're a new mother. This is all brand new, so it's okay to rest a little more."

Resting sounded good, so I lay down next to the

baby and wrapped my arm around him to make sure he didn't find some way to roll off the bed. Ryder walked into the room and stopped dead at the sight of me lying down in the middle of the day, but I smiled to let him know I was all right.

"Okay, Mom. I promise you'll get to see us real soon."

"I know, honey. Stay safe. I love you."

My emotions still a jumbled mess, they bubbled up to the surface when I heard her tell me she loved me. I choked back the tears and smiled. "I love you too. I'll talk to you soon."

After everything I'd been through that day, I took a deep breath in and let it out slowly. Ryder hurried over to the side of the bed and crouched down next to Cayden and me. His face showed as much worry as I felt.

"What happened? Why didn't you go to your mother's today?"

"Because my father has decided that anytime Cayden and I leave the house, we have to be chaperoned by one of his men, if you're not with us."

That look of worry Ryder wore morphed into a far more serious expression as he drew his eyebrows in. "Why? I don't see the reason for it all of a sudden."

"That's what my mother said. She asked me if I thought he knew she and I had been in contact. I told her I don't think so, but who knows? All of this today might have been just to see my reaction to when he said I had to take one of his goons with me wherever I go."

I rolled over and snuggled up to Cayden, who still somehow slept blissfully between his father and me. Taking a deep breath, I inhaled the scent of his hair and loved how pure it smelled as it filled my nose.

"Do you think he knows?" I asked Ryder as he watched the baby and me.

He thought about the question for a moment and then shook his head. "I don't think so. I've made sure that you only go to see her when he and his guys are gone from the estate."

Reaching over Cayden's belly, I slid my hand into Ryder's, desperate for some feeling of security after all that had gone on that day. "But what about the guys who don't leave, like you and Johnson? What about them? Or any of the staff? Maybe one of them has told him about me leaving?"

"I don't think so, Serena. Johnson doesn't seem to care about anything but fishing, and who else does that leave? The cook? The maid? The gardeners? I don't think in the two years I worked for him I saw him talk to any of them more than once, except the cook. They're more loyal to you and me than they are to him. With the way he treats the staff, I wouldn't be surprised if they wouldn't even spit on him if he was on fire."

"Why does he have to do things like this? I just want my mother to see her grandson. Why do I have to sneak around like I'm committing some crime by taking our son to see her?"

Ryder crawled onto the bed and lay down next to Cayden. Leaning over him, he pressed a soft kiss onto my lips. "Because he's a tyrant, and tyrants have to control everyone around them."

"I couldn't stand having him even touch the baby today. I don't know why, but it terrified me. I hated it. Then he started bouncing him up and down so fast that I wanted to scream. I don't know what happened to me when we were in his office, but if I could have, I would have taken Cayden and just run away. I would have gotten into the car and driven as fast as I could as far away as possible."

"For what it's worth, I don't think your father would ever hurt the baby, Serena. Not physically, at least. If anything, he's overprotective of him. He stops into the security room nearly every day to ask me about him. If he's eating right, if I think he's happy with the nursery. I tell him everything's fine, which I think has kept him at bay, for the most part. I just think he's become with Cayden like he used to be with you and then with me."

I looked into his green eyes and saw the fear he

felt at that idea. My father's obsessions never turned out good, especially for the objects of his obsession. I wouldn't let our son become another victim of Robert Erickson's need for control.

"We can't let him do that to him, Ryder."

He cupped my cheek and smiled like everything would be all right. "Don't worry. I'm not going to let that happen."

Like every other time Ryder promised to protect me or our child, I believed him with every fiber of my being. More than anything else, the man protected those he loved. He'd proven that time and time again.

"When do you think I'll be able to take the baby up to see my mother again?"

Ryder bent his head down and kissed the top of Cayden's head. "I don't know when he and his men will be leaving again anytime soon, but the solution to making sure none of his men go with you is me going instead. I'll just have to make sure nobody follows us when we leave."

The prospect of my mother finally getting to spend time with Ryder thrilled me. Except for that night when he got her and Michael away from Jesse, they'd never gotten to know each other. The mere thought of him coming with us next time made the terrible events of that morning fade into a distant memory as I lay there beside him and Cayden.

"I'd love that, Ryder. My mother thinks the world of you, and I know she'd love to see you too. Do you think that can happen soon?"

He wrapped his arm around me and pressed his forehead to mine. "I promise it will happen just as soon as I can be sure it will be safe. Trust me. I'll get you there."

Of all the things I felt for him, none was as strong as the trust I had that he would always be the one to make sure Cayden and I were safe and happy. No matter how hard my father worked to make sure that didn't happen.

Chapter Ten

Ryder

I KNOCKED ON the door and rubbed my hands together, hoping to get rid of some of the dampness. All the way there, I'd grown more and more nervous over meeting Serena's mother. Yeah, we'd met that night when Robert had sent Jesse after her, but tonight was different.

"Hey, what's wrong? Do you think someone saw us?" Serena asked with fear in her eyes.

"No. That's not it. Don't worry. No one saw us. We're okay."

"Then what's wrong? You look like something is wrong, Ryder. Tell me, please."

I hesitated, unsure how to explain what I was feeling, but finally just said it. "It's meeting your mother. I'm a little nervous."

"Why?"

"The first time I met her I was there as one of your father's men. I know what she thinks of them. She has every right to after what Robert's done to her, but I'm worried she's going to think I'm not good enough for you."

I hung my head and said what else was in my mind. "That I am just that stray he thinks I am and you can do better than me."

"Ryder, look at me. Please. This is important."

Lifting my head, I saw a look of pain in her eyes. I hated that. Once again, I'd put that there.

She took my hand and brought it to her mouth to kiss my knuckles. Knuckles that had slammed into the jaws of opponents in the ring and the faces of those men who Robert sent me to rough up. Knuckles that had no place near her gentleness.

I moved my hand to pull it away, but she refused to let go and held tight. "You are not just some stray my father brought home. You are a good man who has never wanted to do anything but protect me. You saved my mother and Michael. You have nothing to be ashamed of. Do you hear me? Nothing. My mother judges people on how they treat her and the ones she loves, and on that, you're the best man in the world."

Cayden made a squealing sound like he wanted to second his mother's comments about me, and I couldn't help but smile. I still worried I wasn't good enough for her, but I wanted to believe I would be someday.

Serena kissed me softly on the lips and whispered, "I love you. All of you. And my mother's going to love you too. You'll see."

The door opened and Alita stood smiling, her arms open to take Cayden into them. "Come in, and let me see that grandson of mine. Did you miss Grandma? Because Grandma missed you."

Happy to go to her, Cayden cooed liked he did whenever he was content. "Is everything okay?" she asked, "Did you have a nice drive here? I know this little guy doesn't like the car so much," Alita said as she ushered us into the house.

"It was fine, Mom. He slept most of the way," Serena said as she slipped her hand into mine. "So I think official introductions are in order."

Alita shifted Cayden from her right arm to her left and smiled. "I don't think it's necessary to introduce us, honey. It's not every day someone saves your life. I don't think I'll ever forget Ryder."

Turning to look up at me, Serena once again brought my hand to her lips in a kiss. "Well, I think it's only right. Mom, this is Ryder, my husband."

I watched to see Alita's reaction, looking for judgment in her expression, but I saw nothing like that when she gave me a warm smile so much like her daughter's. Still holding the baby, she wrapped her arms around me loosely in a hug and kissed my cheek. "It's nice to have you here with us finally, Ryder. You are very welcome to the family."

Serena beamed her happiness, and as Alita

turned away to walk with Cayden to the table in the dining room, I bent down and kissed her. "Thank you. You didn't have to do that."

"Yes, I did. You're the most important person in the world to me, other than our son, who wouldn't exist without you. You've done more to ensure my happiness than anyone else. I'm proud to be able to tell my mother you're my husband."

I doubted we'd get the same reaction if she told her father we'd married. I was good enough to be his son in front of his friends, and I was good enough to be his favorite when it suited him. But I wasn't good enough to be with his daughter, even after jumping through every hoop he put in front of me and doing everything he asked of me.

I'd never be good enough for Robert Erickson, and I hated that.

ALITA HELD CAYDEN in her arms and kissed him on the forehead. "You know, Serena was the best baby. She rarely ever cried, and she always had a smile for me when I took her out of her crib in the morning. I never thought I'd see such a good baby again, but I think this little guy might give her a run for her money."

"He even sleeps through the night already," Serena said with a huge smile. "I can't tell you how much his mother likes that."

"And his father," I chimed in, thrilled to finally have the chance at a full night's sleep after months of waking up in the middle of the night to his crying blaring through the baby monitor.

"He's got such a wonderful disposition," Alita said as she nuzzled his cheek. "Always so happy. That's how you know he's being taken care of. He's happy."

"Was Janelle a good baby too?" Serena asked, piquing my curiosity. She wasn't a good adult, so I wondered where along the way she'd turned rotten or if she'd always been that way.

Pursing her lips, Alita appeared to think about what answer to give, but when her expression turned to look like she'd just tasted a lemon, I knew exactly what Janelle had been since the day she was born.

"Well, good is a relative term."

I nudged Serena's arm with my elbow and chuckled. "I knew it. No way she was as sweet as you were. Ever."

Pretending to scold me, she playfully smacked my arm and scowled. "Stop. Janelle has her moments, but I think she might be coming around lately."

She was referring to her heart-to-heart talk with her sister when she came to visit and dropped the bombshell that her husband had already begun seeing another woman. None of this surprised me, even if it surprised Serena. I barely knew Charles to see him, but if he was any kind of man, being with a woman like Janelle wasn't exactly high on his list of things to do.

"Did something happen?" Alita asked, her motherly concern obvious as the smile slid from her face.

Serena quickly moved to reassure her. "No. Well, yes, but I think it might have been a good thing in the long run. Janelle and Charles aren't really together anymore. He's been seeing another woman for the past few months."

"How is she handling it?"

As Serena tried to find a kind way to explain how Janelle was doing, I thought back to that night of Robert's party when Janelle all but propositioned me as we danced. She hadn't grabbed my cock, for once, but if I'd been interested in getting with her, I had a feeling she wouldn't have given me much resistance.

So her disappointment that her husband was stepping out seemed hypocritical, at least. Typical Janelle. Everything really was all about her.

"I think she's upset. Janelle never had any ridiculous notions about their marriage like they would live happily ever after or anything like that, but I think to her, Charles cheating on her is like him breaking a contract."

Hearing Serena defend her sister like that made me thankful I had never let Janelle's groping go any further. After hearing he had hoped I would end up with Janelle, it seemed Robert would have allowed that. But she definitely wasn't a woman I'd ever want.

She was too much like her father.

Alita's expression changed, and her eyes filled with sadness. Shaking her head, she sighed. "I always hoped your father's world and his warped sense of what was right wouldn't seep into your lives, but that clearly was a pipe dream."

As much as I knew Serena wanted to see the best in her sister, I saw something else. "You might have hoped that, Alita, but Janelle is like Robert. She thinks just like him. Everything has a price, including people and their feelings."

She sighed again and nodded. "That is disappointing, but it's not surprising. I like to think that if I was around, she might have turned out differently. Without me there to show her there was another way, all she saw was her father's."

I wanted to say that even though those words sounded nice, they were a cop out. Janelle was who she was because of her choices. Serena didn't have her mother around and had less time with her when she was in her life, and she turned out nothing like Robert. As much as I was the first to blame him for virtually anything that happened in our lives, he hadn't created that monster in Janelle.

He'd simply encouraged what she was by nature.

I didn't speak up about it, though, because like Serena, her mother preferred to think people were good, overall. How either woman could believe that baffled me. I'd only been a part of Robert's world for a little over two years, and I was surer than I'd ever been that most people possessed little good in their hearts, and what good existed they'd easily trade away for something to benefit them.

A smell I'd grown all too familiar with in the past few months wafted toward my nose, and I reached my hands out to take Cayden. "Someone needs a diaper change right now," I said with a chuckle.

Alita shook her head and held him to her. "No, I'll get it. That's what happens when you go to Grandma's house. It'll give you two a break I'm sure you desperately need."

Instead of just agreeing, Serena stood from her chair and grabbed the diaper bag before heading over to pick up Cayden from her mother's arms. "Actually, let me do it so you and Ryder can talk a little. My little man and I won't be long."

Left alone, we sat in silence for a few moments, but as soon as Alita heard the sound of the bathroom door shutting behind Serena, she leaned over toward me like she'd been waiting to say something and finally the time had come.

I wasn't sure I wanted to hear what she planned to say.

"Ryder, I want you to know I'm very happy Serena has you in her life."

The way she said that sounded so solemn that I didn't know what I should answer in return. Fumbling with my words, I finally said, "I'm the lucky one, Alita. I know that."

Her reaction of shaking her head surprised me. "That's not what I mean. I'm just happy she has someone who will stand up for her with her father. Do you understand?"

I nodded, understanding all too well. Robert saw little need to be kind to his younger daughter on most occasions, and more often than I wished, I felt like I had to remind him that tormenting her wasn't something I could let happen.

Alita had no idea what Serena had been through since losing her all those years ago.

"I would never let anyone hurt her or Cayden. I promise you that."

She reached across the table and patted my hand gently. "I know, and it means the world to me that she has that. I wish my other daughter had the same."

Having nothing nice to say about Janelle and

curious to know how someone like her would ever be with Robert Erickson, I leaned forward and quietly said, "I have to know. How did you and Robert ever get together?"

She took a deep breath in and let it out slowly, like she was thinking back to the good old days. I couldn't imagine any days being good with him in them, so I waited eagerly to hear the story of them.

"Hmmmm…I guess it's next to impossible to see now, but at one time, Robert was the kind of man I respected. He was always driven to succeed, but it wasn't at any cost. He wanted to take over the world, and I loved that about him. He was a man whose passions made him who he was."

All I knew of Robert told me whoever this person was she so fondly remembered existed no more. His only passions now were ruthlessly controlling everyone around him, cheap blondes, and that damn bourbon drink he seemed to have in his hands all the time.

"I've never met the man you describe, Alita. I've been around for two years, but the Robert I know goes after what he wants and doesn't give a damn about who he hurts. That includes his daughters."

"I know," she said sadly, looking off down the hall toward the bathroom. "Serena has suffered particularly at his hands. It's like he knew she was weaker than her sister and took advantage of that."

I winced at her description of Serena as weak. She may have been in the past, but not anymore. Now she didn't let herself be run over by Robert or anyone else. I loved her more than ever for that.

"You know, I can almost remember to the day when he became this person he is now. It was like one night he went to bed and the next day he was different. Nobody mattered anymore."

"When was that?" I wondered aloud, curious to know what could have changed him from the man Alita loved and had two children with to the man who would send her away one night and then try to kill her years later.

She got a faraway look in her eyes and shook her head. "It was when Serena was about five years old. Yeah, that would have made Janelle just about seven. He'd been working on some merger that would have given him tremendous power in the mining industry. I remember he was gone day and night meeting with people about it, and at one point, it looked like the deal would fall through. Overnight, he changed from someone who was definitely driven to someone who became obsessed with power."

I nodded, all too familiar with Robert's obsessions. "Now he's as obsessed with people as he is with power."

She turned to look at me and frowned. "Oh, I know all about his obsessions with people. He's always been like that. He pursued me like a demon. When he sees something or someone he wants, he is single-minded in bringing them into his world. I told Serena to watch him with Cayden. I didn't like hearing how fixated Robert was with you. I'm worried that the obsession he had with Serena and then you has been transferred to your son."

I worried about that too. So far, Robert hadn't been able to spend any real amount of time with our son because he was always with one of us, but after what Serena told me about their meeting in his office the other day, I wondered how long it would be before he tried to have more say in Cayden's life.

But that's where he would find himself up against me because when it came to Serena and my son, I wasn't going to let him control either of them.

"Don't worry. I might not have the money or the power Robert has, but he won't be manipulating Cayden or Serena. Not as long as I'm around."

"I believe you, but please, don't ever let your guard down. And if it seems like you're ever safe with him, that's when you're most at risk."

"I'm a fighter, Alita. I always have been. I won't let Robert hurt my wife or my son. I'd give my life for them to be safe."

Fear filled her eyes, and she quickly shook her head. "They won't be safe if you're not around, Ryder. Don't let that happen."

"Don't worry. I have no intention of letting Robert do anything to us. Not them and not me."

She sighed heavily and turned to look down the hallway as the bathroom door opened. "I swore to myself I'd wait him out. I hate that you two now have to do the same. I wish you didn't have to do that like I have."

As I thought about the one way I knew that would save us from having to wait Robert out, Serena returned to the table with a much cleaner smelling child and handed him back to Alita.

"Sorry that took so long. It was a bit of a mess. For someone who only eats one thing, he sure does have a variety of things happening in his diapers."

Alita held Cayden in front of her and pressed kisses onto his belly. "Who's Grandma's messy little boy?"

He giggled each time she did it, and Serena said, "Cayden is Grandma's messy boy!"

Soon, Cayden opened his mouth to yawn big, a sign it was nearly time to go. "We better get moving to get home," I said, unhappy that we had to leave but knowing we should.

"Already?" Alita asked, hugging the baby to her. "I wish these visits didn't go by so quickly."

"We'll come again soon, Mom. I promise," Serena said with a smile as she grabbed the diaper bag from the back of her chair. "Cayden needs to get to sleep, so he wouldn't be much fun to be around in a few minutes anyway. I see crying in our future if we don't get him home soon."

Kissing his nose, Alita smiled. "I wouldn't care if all he did was cry. I'd still love to be with him."

We all got up to head toward the door, and after kissing Cayden and Serena goodbye, she turned to me and whispered, "Remember what I said about him. Never let your guard down."

"I won't. I've learned that lesson before with him. Stay safe, and don't let anyone in. If you run into any problems, just call the number you've been using, okay?"

She kissed my cheek and pulled me to her in a hug I hadn't expected. "Thank you for everything, Ryder. I sleep better at night knowing you're taking care of those two precious souls."

As she stepped back, I tried to reassure her. "I will always protect them, Alita. You and Michael too."

"Stay safe and bring them back to me soon, okay? I'll be counting the minutes."

Chapter Eleven

Serena

A S MUCH AS I wanted to take the baby to see my mother again soon, days passed without my father leaving the estate, except to pay a late-night visit to whatever whore he frequented now, and then those days turned into weeks. Because I refused to follow his edict about letting one of his goon squad accompany me whenever I left the grounds without Ryder, for nearly a month, Cayden and I were stuck at home.

Feeling particularly trapped one sunny morning in early summer, I dressed the baby in a blue and green outfit with baseballs and bats on it and laid him in the stroller for a walk around the grounds. It wasn't much and it wasn't anywhere as good as leaving to see my mother, but I'd take it over spending all day cooped up in the house.

It had been years since I walked the full length of the estate. I'd been a teenage girl the last time I explored past the main house and the gardens, but there were acres of land past those. Much of it wasn't anywhere I could take a stroller, but the road that travelled throughout the main part of the estate gave me a long enough walk so I didn't have to return inside for hours.

Cayden smiled up at me as I pushed the stroller around the garage, the concrete smooth enough for him that he didn't get jostled around too much. I leaned down and tickled his uncovered toes until he giggled.

"We don't have to stay in that house, now do we? No, we don't. We're just going to take a walk around and I'll give you the tour. Don't worry. I'll be sure to point out the highlights."

He looked at me with his dark green eyes so much like his father's, and even though I knew he didn't understand a word I'd said, his expression said he liked hearing them anyway. I'd never realized how happy I could be as a mother, but now as he watched me like I was the best thing in the world, I couldn't imagine my life without him. He brought out all the best parts of me I'd only known before with Ryder.

We rolled past the apartments my father's men and the staff lived in, and I stopped in front of the one that used to be Ryder's. Leaning into the stroller, I pushed back the canopy and said to Cayden, "That's where Daddy used to live when he was one of my father's men."

The words left my mouth and I instantly regretted saying them. I never wanted our son to know about what Ryder did for my father. He was a better man than that. He deserved to be known as that man instead of the monster my father had worked so hard to make him.

I pulled the canopy down again to shield Cayden from the sun and began pushing the stroller again. As we passed the apartment I'd shared with Oliver, I said nothing and barely gave it a second glance. My son never needed to know what happened there.

We headed toward the back of the estate where my father had his own townhouse. Far enough away from the main house to be private, it still stood way too close for my comfort on most days. Much bigger than the apartments for his employees, it was actually the size of three of their places put together.

I saw it in the distance as we approached and couldn't help but compare it to the tiny carriage house he'd forced my mother to live in for all those years and the rundown house in a strange town she had to live in now to hide away from him.

Someday that would change. All of this would change, and he wouldn't have the power anymore.

Cayden began to fuss, so I slowed down my pace and turned around before I reached my father's house. I had no reason to go there anyway.

"What do you say we take a walk in the garden,

my little man?" I asked Cayden, who smiled up at me like he knew exactly what I'd said and loved the idea.

I followed the road to the back of the house and the entrance to the gardens. The path wasn't exactly meant for a baby stroller, but we'd make do.

"It's just a little bumpy for a few minutes until Mommy gets us to my favorite spot of all, so be patient with me, okay?"

My question received a smile in return, and in a few minutes I'd rolled him to the place in the garden where Ryder and I liked to meet last summer. The rose bush next to the bench sat in full bloom, and the fragrance from the flowers filled the air with sweetness.

Reaching into the stroller, I lifted Cayden out and sat him on my lap to enjoy the beautiful day, making sure to put his little hat on to protect his head from the sun. He quickly grew tired and rested his head against my chest, so I closed my eyes and let myself enjoy the contentment I felt sitting there with my son in a place his father and I loved and my mother had created years before.

I didn't know how long I sat there with Cayden in my arms, but I felt the sun disappear at one point and opened my eyes, excitedly thinking Ryder had taken a break from work and found us there in our special spot.

But I didn't see Ryder. Instead, I saw my father

standing in front of me blocking the light. Instantly, I clutched the baby to me and sat up straight on the bench.

"What are you doing out here, Dad? You never come this far back in the garden."

He stood in his dark suit and grey tie staring down at me and arched a single eyebrow. "The better question is what are you doing here, Serena?"

Already frustrated by the early questions of his inquisition, I held onto Cayden tightly and shrugged as if his presence didn't upset me. "Enjoying the day with my son. Or am I under the Robert Erickson version of house arrest and I can't even go outside?"

His face twisted into a grimace, but he didn't leave. Instead, he sat down beside me and said nothing, like we were the kind of father and daughter who could spend quiet time together and neither of us would feel like it was a matter of waiting for the next shoe to drop.

We weren't, and I sat waiting, wishing he would just leave me alone.

Finally, when he did begin to speak, it was to give his opinion on how I was doing as a mother. "I wish you would hire a nanny for the baby, Serena."

"I don't want a nanny. I don't work, so why shouldn't I take care of my son?" I said, my defensiveness rising with every word.

With a wave of his hand, he dismissed my ideas.

"Even your mother had a nanny, Serena."

I turned to look at him to see if I could find any evidence in his face that his claim was true. I saw nothing to show he was lying, but he had to be because I didn't remember ever having a nanny.

"That's not true. Who?"

"She did. Her name was Cynthia. You and your sister loved her when you were babies."

"How long did she work for us?"

He thought about the question for a moment and shook his head. "She left before you were a year old. Your mother felt she didn't need her around, for some reason."

His dismissive tone whenever he spoke about my mother, like she wasn't worthy of the respect I knew she deserved, irritated me. I wanted to tell him if my mother thought she didn't need a damn nanny, then she didn't need one. She probably caught him sleeping with the woman.

What would he know about taking care of babies anyway? I don't remember him any more during those years than I remembered the nanny.

But I remembered my mother from then.

I looked off in the distance, not caring if he even heard me reminisce about her. "Mom used to sit with Janelle and me in the kitchen and try to teach us how to make cinnamon sugar toast. We used to make a mess all over the counter, but she always looked so happy, no matter what we did to the kitchen."

"It's a shame she won't get the chance to see her grandson grow up."

Cayden began to cry, so I rubbed his back for a minute to calm him since I knew it wasn't time for him to eat again. My father's cryptic words hung in the air, but even though I wanted to tell him she would, I said nothing. We both knew he'd ordered her killed and Jesse had failed because of Ryder. It existed as an unspoken truth among the three of us.

When I didn't take the bait, he turned toward me and took Cayden's hand in his. "I'm so happy you and Ryder are doing so well. I wasn't sure he'd be able to come back from everything and be the man he'd need to be for you two."

Before I could stop myself, my curiosity got the best of me and I asked, "Come back from what?"

My father frowned and shook his head, like he was disappointed. "I would have thought he'd have told you."

Holding Cayden to me, I tried not to focus on my father's hand still holding his. "I'm sure he has, but your statement was so vague."

He brought the baby's hand to his mouth to kiss his fingertips and looked up at me. "I want you to know, Serena, that I did it because I love you."

"Did what?"

Sitting up straight, he let Cayden's hand drop. "Cleaned up that mess with that fighter. I'm sure Ryder didn't mean to beat him into a coma, but the police weren't going to care about his intentions."

Suddenly, Ryder's drinking and nightmares made sense. He'd been suffering through that all alone for months, with no one to confide in about what he was going through.

But I didn't want my father to think there were any secrets between Ryder and me.

"I've wanted to thank you for doing that for us, Dad. Ryder told me all about it, and I know you may not have liked the idea of us being together, so you helping him when he needed it to stay with me and be there for our son means a lot to me."

My father stood from the bench and flashed one of his crocodile smiles. "That's what family does for one another, honey."

I pasted a smile on my face and watched as he walked away, clearly pleased with how our little conversation had gone. He knew Ryder had never told me, but what he thought would happen next wouldn't. Maybe those bimbos he liked to spend time with yelled and screamed at a man when they found out he'd hidden something, but I knew Ryder too well for that.

He didn't tell me because he wanted to protect me. My father banked on me being like his women, but I was nothing like them.

Even though I grew up without my mother, I was her daughter, not his.

I tucked Cayden into bed and turned on his nightlight before checking to make sure the baby monitor was working properly. Exhausted from our time outside earlier that day, he didn't even fuss for a few minutes like usual before falling right to sleep.

Ryder came into the nursery just as I said goodnight to Cayden for the last time. I put my finger up to my lips to let him know he'd already fallen fast asleep.

"He's tired from our adventure outside today," I whispered.

Craning his neck to look into the crib, Ryder smiled. "He looks so peaceful. I'd give anything to sleep like that just once a week."

I wove my fingers through his and tugged him toward the door. "Let's go. He needs to sleep."

We got out into the hall and I closed the door behind me. Ryder stood staring at me like something was on his mind.

"Why did you rush me out of there?"

I planted a kiss on his lips and smiled. "I didn't rush you out. It's just that the baby is tired. We had a big day today."

"A big day? Doing what? I know you didn't leave

the estate, so what did you do on your big day?" he asked as we walked toward our room.

"How do you know I didn't leave today?" I asked with a giggle, knowing full well that as head of security he knew the exact whereabouts of everyone on the property at all times.

He recognized my teasing and slid his arms around my waist as we walked into our room. Resting his chin on my shoulder as I walked, he explained, "Well, other than the fact that I know everything that happens on this estate, I also know how you feel about taking one of Robert's men along with you when you go anywhere."

I turned in his hold and looked up at him, stopping next to the bed. "I guess that was a stupid question then, huh? In my defense, I was teasing more than anything else."

A slow grin spread across his lips, making him look incredibly sexy. "Teasing? So you want to tease tonight?"

Sliding my hands down the front of his shirt, I let them come to rest just above his pants and felt the hardness of his abs against my palms. God, I could spend the rest of my life exploring the pleasures of his body.

"I'm not against teasing any time," I said quietly as I stretched my thumbs out to slide under the waist of his pants.

I brushed against the head of his cock and looked up at him. "Are you?"

His tongue slid across his bottom lip before he winced. Need filled his eyes as he said, "Nope. As long as the teasing is followed by something a little more satisfying."

The tips of my thumbs traced up the sides of his cock, making him wince again. "Like?"

He fastened his hands around my wrists and held them in place as he pushed his hips forward to make my thumbs press harder against his skin. "Like your mouth on my cock or my cock in your pussy. Either one...or both...both sounds better, to be honest."

I strained against his hold, tugging my arms to no avail. Looking up, I pursed my lips. "I can't do anything as long as you're keeping my hands from what they want."

He released my wrists and watched as I unbuttoned his pants before doing the same to his shirt. My breath caught in my chest at the sight of him beneath his clothes. Hard and toned, his body never ceased to make me want him.

Running my hands over the muscular peaks and valleys of his abs, I teased him with a light touch that made goosebumps rise up on his skin. A thin trail of black hair from just below his belly button ran down behind his pants, and I followed it with my fingertip until it met his erect cock.

"I'm just about done with the teasing," he groaned and closed his eyes.

I lowered myself to my knees and wrapped my hand around his thick cock. "Then I guess I better get to the satisfying part."

He opened his eyes and watched me wrap my lips around the head before slowly sliding down his shaft, my tongue flicking the skin underneath as I took all of him into my mouth. Seeing him stare down at me as I sucked his cock always excited me, and I felt my panties get wet in anticipation of when I'd have him inside me.

Wrapping his hand around the base, he fed his cock to me, setting the pace as I swallowed every inch of him and then slowly eased him out until all that was left between my lips was the head. I knew what he loved, and I gave it to him.

"Oh…God, baby…you feel so fucking good…" he moaned while he stared at me through half-lidded eyes.

I took hold of him and began stroking, but he shook his head and pulled me up to my feet. "I don't want to come like that. We're still working on giving Cayden a baby brother or sister."

He kissed me hard on the mouth, snaking his tongue in to tease mine as he quickly stripped my clothes off. In seconds, I stood naked in front of him and desperate to feel him inside me.

His hand tugged at my hair, pulling my head back so I had no choice but to look up at him when he spoke. "I want to see your face when I slide into you, Serena. I want to watch your eyes fill with that look you get when my cock is inside you."

"Fuck me, Ryder," I whimpered, willing to beg if I had to.

Lifting me to waist level, he held me by my hips and groaned, "Wrap your legs around me."

I did as he ordered and kept my eyes focused on his while he slowly eased his cock into me, inch by delicious inch until he was buried in me completely. He stretched my body to take all of him, a feeling more exquisite than anything else I'd ever felt in my life.

Then, just when I thought I couldn't feel any more incredible, he tilted his hips and began fucking me in earnest. I rocked against him, desperate to feel him inside me when he moved away and beyond happy when his cock touched that spot deep inside me that caused pleasure to race through my body.

He buried his face in my shoulder and moved us toward the bed, moaning my name as he lowered me down onto my back without leaving my body. I pressed my heels hard into the small of his back and silently urged him to fuck me harder.

Hovering over me, he planted his forearms on

either side of my head and kissed me long and deep as he slid in and out of my pussy. Slow strokes gave way to faster stabs into my body, and he grunted with each plunge into me.

"Come for me, baby. Come for me and let me feel your cunt tighten around my cock."

My nails scratched across his shoulder blades, and I arched my back as the first moments of my orgasm began. Ryder sensed I was close and bore down, fucking me hard.

In his ear, I pleaded, "Don't stop. Fuck me. Fill me up."

He looked down at me and winced. "Fuck, I can't hold back when you talk like that."

Tugging his hair hard, I came and moaned, "Don't hold back. I want to feel you come, Ryder."

I got my wish a few seconds later, and he collapsed on top of me, his sweat-drenched body pressing against mine. Thoroughly exhausted, we said nothing for a few minutes as we recuperated from our lovemaking, both of us completely satisfied.

Finally, he lifted his head and kissed me softly on the lips. "No one would believe such a pretty mouth could say such filthy things. I love it."

"Only for you."

Propping his head up on his hand, he kissed me again and whispered against my lips, "Everything for you, Serena."

He closed his eyes and a smile formed on his lips, making him look even sexier. I loved him, and even though it wasn't the best timing, I quietly said, "I know about what happened to that fighter, Ryder."

His eyes opened wide and he stared in confusion at me for a moment. Finally, with an expression that looked like he was in pain, he said, "Who told you?"

"My father. He found me with Cayden out in the garden today and seemed all too eager to tell me because he thought I didn't know. I tried to pretend like it wasn't a secret, but I think he knew you hadn't told me."

Ryder hung his head and sighed. "I'm sorry, Serena. It wasn't meant as a lie, if that's what you're thinking."

"Oh no! That's not what I was thinking at all," I said, cradling his face so he would look at me. "I just felt terrible that you were dealing with that all on your own. Is that what the nightmares have been about?"

He nodded. "Yes and no. I don't like that he used that to try to cause problems between us. He's never going to let us be together and be happy, is he?"

Pressing my forehead to his, I reminded him of the truth of who we were to each other. "I'm your wife and you're my husband, Ryder. He can't stop us from being together because we're together without the need for anyone's permission. And we don't need him to be happy. We have our own happiness with each other and Cayden."

He smiled and kissed me. "I know, but I hate that he thinks he can cause problems between us like that. He's never going to let up."

I rolled him onto his back and curled up against his body, resting my head on his shoulder like I used to when we lay in the bed together right after he came to the estate all that time ago. "He's going to be who he is, and I'm not sure there's anything we can do about that other than stay clear of him and keep our son away from him. My father's day of reckoning is coming. I have no doubt about that."

Ryder wrapped his arm around me and held me close. "I hope you're right."

I did too.

Chapter Twelve

Ryder

"We're out of diapers."

Those four words were the last thing I wanted to hear Serena whisper to me in the middle of the night. I would have preferred to hear her say, "Take me now, Ryder," or anything else related to something I wanted to do at two a.m. instead of giving me the news I had to get up, get dressed, and drive to the only store open at this time of night ten miles away.

I opened my eyes to see her standing by the side of the bed with a completely naked Cayden dangling from her arms, his penis aimed straight at my head. Scrubbing the sleep from my face, I rolled over to avoid the possibility of a direct hit.

"I get that we're out of diapers, but why are you aiming him at me like that?" I asked into the pillow.

"Oh, I wasn't thinking. I just wanted to give him a chance to air out a bit until you got back with them," she said with a chuckle.

How she could be so cute minutes after being so

rudely awakened baffled me. Sliding out of bed, I walked over to where I'd thrown my pants hours before.

"You know, since both of us are naked, you should be too," I joked as I held the pants out in front of me so I could step into them.

She raised her eyebrows and shook her head. "You're not naked anymore. Be sure to get the right size this time and get the ones with the special leg holes that give him room to move."

All this flowed into my brain and got trapped between the sleep that still ruled there and my intense desire to not be putting on a shirt to make a diaper run. "Got it. Size medium with nice legs."

Serena walked toward me and stopped to kiss me on the cheek. "It sounds like you're ordering a woman."

I kissed her and kissed Cayden, who was wide awake and squirming in her arms. "I already have a woman, and she's got great legs, by the way. I'd like it if they were wrapped around me."

"Shhhh. Not in front of the baby," she chastised me, covering my son's ears.

Opening my eyes wide, I bent down and looked at Cayden. "You know, he doesn't understand what we say. I could tell him that I'm pretty damn pissed off about having to go out in the middle of the night for his diapers and he wouldn't know a thing if I kept this cheery voice going the whole time."

"Don't be cranky."

Cayden reached out his chubby little hand to grab my nose, adding insult to injury, and I stood up to face Serena giving me her irritated look. "And you want to have more kids?" I asked, unsure at that moment how I felt about the idea.

"Lots more," she answered in that sweet voice that either meant she loved me or she wanted to kill me because I hadn't gotten back with the diapers yet.

"Maybe we could get a nanny, if that's the case? You know, someone who could drive in the middle of the night for diapers or maybe even someone whose job it is to make sure we never run out?"

"No nanny," she said, frowning.

Clearly, that conversation would have to wait until I had my wits about me. For now, I'd table that discussion and do what I had to.

Get the diapers.

"I'll be right back. Cayden, hold it in, buddy."

"Love you," Serena said sweetly. "Be careful."

THE GROCERY STORE at two a.m. was full of sleepy fathers and drunks. At least that's how it seemed as I roamed the aisles looking for those roomy leg-holed size medium diapers for my son. I hadn't asked Serena, but as I shuffled my tired body toward the baby section, I had to wonder why anyone who couldn't even walk yet would need more room to move. How much room did he need to lay there?

I headed down the diaper and baby wipes aisle and felt the presence of someone behind me. Something told me it wasn't another half-awake father on a diaper run, so I turned around and saw the two FBI agents from the parking garage. They weren't dressed in their usual dark suit look, but even wearing street clothes, they stuck out like sore thumbs in a suburban store in the middle of the night.

"Did you two piss someone off to get hours like this?" I asked as I headed toward the diaper selection.

They said nothing but still continued to follow me. I grabbed a package of size medium diapers with the leg holes just like Serena wanted and turned back around to face them again.

"Has it crossed your minds that you look pretty obvious following me through the aisles of the store in the middle of the night?"

The one who'd given me his card stared straight ahead and said flatly, "We're hoping someone notices and tells Erickson."

Looking around to see if anyone had noticed, I saw no one else. "You think he's having someone tail me? You don't understand how he thinks. I'm one of the two people who just gave him a grandson. You guys haven't done your homework."

In all honesty, I had wondered myself if Robert had been having me followed. He knew Alita was still in hiding somewhere and I'd helped her to safety, so he probably had assigned at least one of his guys to tail me.

And my bullshit claim to these FBI guys that I was in the clear because Serena and I had given him a grandson wasn't anything I believed. He'd have me killed in a second if it suited him.

It simply hadn't yet.

"How's this sound for homework? You were basically homeless living in Erickson's warehouse in Baltimore fighting in the underground fight circuit he runs when he found you and took you to that estate you live on now. You remained as a fighter until he had another fighter beat you so badly you ended up in the hospital. Caught you doing something you weren't supposed to be doing, right?"

I didn't appreciate this FBI fuck giving me the sad rundown of my life as I stood there wishing I was home in bed next to my wife. "So you know some things. Good for you."

Turning to leave, I heard him continue with the history lesson of my life.

"After you recovered from that beating, you went to work for Erickson as one of his men. Nice job there, by the way. Beating guys up, threatening people, even some killing. I'll tell you what, Ryder. The mafia's got nothing on you and Erickson."

I wanted to ignore him, but as we reached the end of the aisle and more customers appeared in front of me, I stopped and walked back toward him.

"So what do you want from me?" I asked, knowing the answer.

"Then there's the prostitution, which you had no direct part in, except for the girl. What's her name? Kitty? But that relationship ended the second Erickson's daughter came back, didn't it? Hell hath no fury like a woman scorned. Isn't that how the old adage goes?"

Was he saying Kitty was working with the FBI against Robert? I took a step back as my brain processed the possibility.

"So you got a stripper to talk to you. Did they teach you that in FBI school, guys? Go after the weakest link? I could have told you Kitty would tell her tale of woe to anyone who'd listen."

The usually quiet FBI guy stepped toward me and shook his head. "She's not the weak link. Want me to continue?"

"Can I stop you?" I asked, feeling particularly smart ass standing there in front of the strained peas.

"But the relationship with Erickson's daughter is a confusing one, Ryder. Maybe you can clear some things up for us. You see, you're definitely a bad guy in this whole thing, but she's nothing like her father and you."

Rage built up inside me from how he spoke about Serena. "No, she's not. And stop talking about her. Now."

"She's obviously in love with you, although I'm having a hard time figuring out why. So now you two have a baby and you're married. You've become everything your father-in-law could ever want in a son, wouldn't you say?"

"If that were the case, why would he have me followed? I think you need to go back and think this through a little more. I expect better from the Feds, though. You guys are slipping."

My cockiness got under his skin, and he quickly said, "How about that fighter you beat into a coma up in West Virginia? How's our thinking on that one?"

A rush of fear washed over me. I should have known Robert didn't have the power to cover up my beating of Justin. And unlike everything else I'd done for him, there was proof of my guilt anyone with an ax to grind could find to put me away for what I'd done out there.

And when they did, there went my life with Serena and Cayden.

As that possibility settled into my brain, my chest began to ache. I couldn't live without them.

"Why don't you just arrest me then?"

The other FBI guy took a deep breath in and let it out slowly as he looked at his partner. Turning to face me, he said, "We don't want you. We want Erickson. And you're the one who's going to give him to us."

So that's how it was going to go. I could stay with the devil, or I could jump into the deep blue sea.

"You're asking me to do something that's probably going to get me killed."

"We're offering you a choice."

"What choice?"

"We can always make sure the police in that small West Virginia town decide that you should pay for your crime. You hold your future and your family's future entirely in your hands."

My future would be lost if Robert found out I was working with the FBI against him. He'd have me killed and then what I'd feared would happen to Serena and Cayden would come true.

He'd make sure she became some other man's wife and my son would be brought up as another man's child. The mere thought of either of those things happening made my stomach churn so much I wanted to throw up.

"All I want to do is stay with my wife and son, and you're not giving me any good choices here.

Either he kills me or you send me away. That's pretty much the situation, right?"

My dilemma didn't seem to affect either one of the men in front of me. They looked like I'd just recited a shopping list, not explained the grim realities of my situation.

"We don't think he'll kill you, to be honest, so that's probably not part of the equation," the FBI guy who seemed to dislike me more said matter-of-factly.

"Equation? This isn't fucking math, man. This is my life. My wife's life. My infant son's life. Our happiness I'm talking about here. You want me to turn on the one person who would kill me for doing that. The only numbers I know in that situation are the two shots to my fucking head that are going to happen when he finds out."

"Then don't help us get Erickson and go down for any number of the crimes you've committed, including the assault in West Virginia."

They didn't offer a whole lot of options. The devil or the deep blue sea. Take it or leave it, and by the way, if you take it, you're putting your life in danger. No fucking big deal.

I had nothing to say to the threat, so they began walking away, but as the one who gave me his card passed me, he said in a low voice, "He's going down, Ryder. You seem like you've turned over a new leaf because of your wife and your son. Don't you want to keep that life? Protect it with everything you could? Would they want you to go down with him?"

That question I knew the answer to. Serena would want me to choose her and Cayden. I wanted to choose them. Fuck, they were everything to me. I loved them more than life itself.

But if I turned on Robert and it didn't go as the FBI believed it would, I'd be a dead man walking. It wouldn't matter where we went. If Robert was still free, he'd see to it I paid for the betrayal I knew would finally be too much for him to forgive.

For the first time, I began to think I might have to do as they wanted. That time of reckoning I'd always trusted would come for Robert had come for me too. I could either save myself and the ones I loved, or I could go down with him, the man who was responsible for every good and bad thing I had in my life now.

SERENA SAT CURLED up and fast asleep in the rocking chair in Cayden's nursery. Wearing shorts and one of my t-shirts, she looked like the girl I met that first night in Robert's office.

Innocent. Sweet. Gentle.

Her tanned legs hung off the front of the chair, her feet bare as always since getting away from Oliver. I watched as her bottom lip poked out in a tiny pout like Cayden made when he slept and couldn't help love how cute she looked.

I looked down into Cayden's crib and saw him staring up at me, wide-eyed and naked, just like I'd left him nearly an hour before. Feeling the sheet around him, I found it dry, thankfully, and picked him up into my arms.

"You know, I didn't really expect you to hold it in, but thanks," I joked as I placed him on the changing table.

He kicked his legs out one and then the another, and I had the sense he was getting ready to let loose, so I quickly ripped the diaper package open and threw a diaper across him so I didn't end up drenched in baby pee. I'd had a bad enough night so far. I didn't need that too.

"Take it easy, little guy. You have to learn to control that thing. Don't let it control you, or you'll regret it for the rest of your life."

He looked up at me with those dark green eyes of his and smiled as he proceeded to soak the diaper while I held it over him. At least he waited so he didn't soak his dad.

"Satisfied now? I guess I should be impressed. You waited a long time there," I said as I folded the diaper and tossed it into the trash.

Grabbing a second one, I held it under my arm while I wiped him clean, and in seconds, he was wearing a new diaper with the roomy leg holes. I didn't place him back in his crib, but instead walked him over to the window to look out.

He made a loud squealing noise I was afraid would wake his mother, but she slept right through it. "Hey, let's keep it down, okay? Mommy's sleeping."

As if he understood me, he turned toward the window and focused his attention quietly on the scene outside. His nursery overlooked the part of the estate that had nothing but grass, but in the distance I thought I could see the mountains there in the dark.

I pointed and tapped on the window. "Someday you, Mommy, and me are going to be far away from here. Maybe in the mountains up there. What do you think of that?"

He bumped his head off mine when I turned to see how he liked that idea, so I kissed him and pulled him close before he started to cry. "It's okay, little man. We're going to be okay. I promise."

When he stopped crying, he opened his mouth wide to yawn. I placed him back in his crib and pulled up the blanket to cover his legs. "And I want you to know I'm going to be around to see you grow up. You can count on that. Somebody's got to be the one to lay down the law, and I think we both know it won't be your mother. You've already got her wrapped around your finger. Nope, it's going to have to be me, so you better believe I'm going to be around to do that for you."

Cayden's eyelids slowly fluttered closed, and within seconds, he was fast asleep like his mother a few feet away. I left him lying there peaceful and looking like an angel and took Serena in my arms to carry her back to bed.

Just before I reached our room, she opened her eyes and asked in a groggy voice, "Did you put a diaper on Cayden?"

"I got it covered. He's dry and fast asleep already."

Happy to hear that, she curled up in my arms and lay her head on my shoulder. "Good. Thank you."

By the time we reached the bed, she had fallen back to sleep, so I gently set her down and covered her legs with the blanket. I stripped out of my clothes and slid under the covers next to her, pulling her close because I needed the feel of her body next to mine.

Everything those FBI guys said repeated in my mind as I lay there with her in my arms. I couldn't lose her and our son. Whatever I had to do to keep them safe and keep me with them I'd do, but every time I tried to convince myself that I could turn on Robert after all he'd done to us, one thing kept coming up to haunt me.

If he found out about my turning on him for the FBI, he'd kill me for certain, but what would he do to Serena? I'd thought he would simply marry her off to another man who could benefit his business, but I'd forgotten about one important thing.

His obsession with Cayden.

Now I feared he'd marry her off to someone else and take our son from her to raise him on his own, just as he had done with her and Janelle when he sent Alita away.

Could I risk that happening and undoubtedly crushing Serena when it did? She'd never recover from the loss of Cayden after losing me.

I closed my eyes to force back the tears at the reality in front of me now. I couldn't gamble on that future never happening, but what choice did I have? Either I did as the FBI wanted and risked Robert ruining all three of our lives, or I let them send me away and the same thing would happen.

It wasn't a choice between the devil and the deep blue sea. It was no choice at all. Either way, Serena and Cayden might be hurt, and I'd be the one to blame.

My past had finally caught up with me. Now it was just a matter of who would suffer because of it.

Chapter Thirteen

Ryder

THE SOUND OF a police siren woke me from a deep sleep, and I bolted straight up in bed, barely awake but terrified. My heart slammed into my ribs at the fear that after my meeting with those agents just a few hours before, I'd set my future in stone.

I turned to my left and saw an empty spot where Serena would normally be. Did she get up to take care of Cayden? I hadn't heard the baby monitor make any noise. Was she in the shower?

Thoughts of how to protect Serena and Cayden raced through my mind. They'd have to leave immediately. Robert would try to stop her from taking the baby away, but if I created enough chaos as they arrested me, she might be able to get away.

Fuck! Why didn't I tell her about the bank account I've been filling with every spare dime? How will I get all that information down before they take me away?

I leapt from the bed and searched frantically for

my clothes. What the fuck had I done with my clothes when I got back from the store? I couldn't find them, so I just grabbed a shirt and pants from the hamper and threw them on, desperate to find Serena before the police got me.

The shower wasn't running and the bathroom was empty, so I ran down the hallway to the nursery and found her on the floor with the baby playing peekaboo with him. It never failed to make me smile when I watched her cover her eyes and Cayden looked up at her with worry in his eyes because she seemed to disappear before she showed him she was still there with him and squealed, "Peekaboo! Mommy's here!"

She turned around and smiled sweetly at me. "Look who came to visit, Cayden? Daddy's here!"

I hurriedly picked up my son and held him in my arms as Serena stood from the floor, clearly not understanding why I'd interrupted their game of peekaboo. She touched my arm, and I looked down at her to see confusion in her eyes.

How the hell would I get to say everything I needed to before they came for me?

"Ryder, what's wrong? You look like you've seen a ghost. What's going on?" she asked in a voice full of fear.

I cradled Cayden's head and kissed him on the cheek before turning to face her. "I need you to know some things before…"

The rest of my words got trapped in my throat as the baby pushed his tiny fingers against my face and made babbling sounds like the feel of my morning stubble amused him. Damnit, I needed to get my head together and keep my fucking emotions under control so she knew what I had to tell her.

"Did something happen? What's wrong, Ryder?" Serena asked, clinging to my forearm as she waited for me to explain.

The look of desperate fear in her eyes made my chest ache. How could I go on living if she wasn't by my side?

"I've done a lot of bad things, Serena…" I began and then the words got lost.

"Ryder, I know what you've done. You're not that person now. What's this all about? Did you have another one of those nightmares?"

Quickly, I hatched a plan. It was stupid and careless, but if that's what it had to be to keep her and Cayden in my life, then that's the way it had to be.

"We need to hurry. Get the baby dressed and then get yourself ready. Nothing too elaborate. Just a few necessities."

Serena shook her head in disbelief. "What? You aren't even wearing shoes, Ryder. Why do we need to go somewhere now? What's going on?"

"We just have to go. I'll explain later. Right now, we have to leave here," I said as I laid Cayden down on the changing table to get him dressed.

I grabbed a pair of shorts and a t-shirt and began wrestling with him to get them on his body. Serena stood next to me staring at us and shaking her head.

Turning to look at her, I pointed at the stack of diapers I'd just brought home a few hours earlier. "We're going to need those, so stuff as many as you can into his diaper bag. Actually, just go get dressed. I can handle things in here."

She placed her hand on mine to stop me. "Tell me what's wrong. Don't leave me in the dark. I'm not some child. I can handle whatever you have to tell me."

"We don't have time for this, Serena!" I yelled, frightening her and Cayden.

A look of pure hurt settled into her face as the baby began crying. I hung my head while regret for what I'd done coursed through me. I just wanted to get us away from this place before the police took me away. I never meant to upset her or Cayden.

"I'm sorry. I didn't mean to yell. We just need to get away from here before everything goes bad."

Gently, she rubbed my back. "What do you mean? What's going to go bad? What happened?"

The sound of footsteps outside in the hallway made my body stiffen, and I pulled Serena close. I hadn't moved fast enough, and now they were at the door. I'd refused to turn on Robert, and the FBI did just what they said they could.

I'd lived on borrowed time for months, and now that was all about to end.

Pressing a kiss to the top of Serena's head, I whispered, "I'm sorry. I never meant for any of this to happen. I have an account at Sun Bank. The account number is written on a piece of paper I hid in the back of my sock drawer. I put a checkbook in the box you put all the stuff from the hospital on the shelf in Cayden's closet. There's enough in the account to help you for a while. I'm sorry I couldn't do more. I really am, Serena."

She looked up at me and I saw the tears well in her eyes. "Why are you telling me this? Are you leaving me? Why? Why would you leave me and Cayden?"

A knock at the door made my blood run cold, and I held her tightly to me. "I love you, Serena. I don't want to go. I hope you know that."

I heard the door open and turned around to see Robert standing in the doorway. Studying his expression, I found nothing to say he felt the least bit upset about me being hauled away for what I'd done.

"Ryder, I need to speak to you alone."

I didn't know what he wanted to talk to me about or how he'd gotten the police to wait until we had this conversation, but I couldn't keep hiding out in my son's nursery. I needed to face the consequences for what I'd done.

Looking down at Serena, I hated seeing the sadness in her eyes. I'd put that sadness there. I'd never meant to hurt her like this. Fuck, that was the last thing I ever wanted to do. I was supposed to protect her from being hurt. Now I was the reason for that look in her eyes.

I held her by the shoulders and took a deep breath before I whispered, "Remember what I said about Sun Bank. Take care of Cayden, and get away from here as soon as you can, okay?"

She opened her mouth to say something, but I just shook my head. I didn't want Robert knowing Serena might have a way to finally escape from this place.

I gave Cayden one last kiss as my emotions began to unravel inside me. Christ, I might never see him again. "I'm sorry, bud. I didn't mean for this to happen."

Then without looking at Serena because I knew I wouldn't be able to handle it, I turned and followed Robert out into the hallway. I stopped dead at the stairs when I didn't see any police waiting for me. He said nothing and silently walked to his office, so I did the same.

I found him standing at the bar making a drink.

Since it was barely nine o'clock in the morning on a Saturday, it seemed strange that he'd already be drinking his bourbon and branch. Maybe he was toasting my leaving.

"Where are they?" I asked, looking around his office for where he had them waiting.

He turned around and shook his head. "Who?"

"The cops, Robert. I heard the sirens before when they came onto the estate," I said, nervously clutching the back of one of those red leather chairs.

Once he finished making his drink, he slowly walked to his desk and sat down in his chair. He extended his arm to offer me a seat and tilted the glass up to his lips.

"Sit."

I did as he ordered and waited impatiently for the news of when the cops would swoop in and take me away. He seemed disinterested in saying much of anything, though, and simply stared straight ahead for nearly a minute before turning his focus to me.

"My wife is dead. They found her this morning."

I realized I'd been sitting up perfectly straight and holding my breath, and now I sagged against the back of the chair as a mixture of relief and utter sadness threatened to overwhelm me. Alita was dead. That's what the police had been there about. Not to take me away but to tell him she was dead.

"How? How did this happen?"

He shrugged. "A home invasion in the middle of the night. The young man who lived with her was found dead too."

My mouth dropped open, and I sat there in shock as what he said sunk in. He'd killed her. He'd found her even after I tried so hard to keep where she was a secret and killed her and Michael.

Had I been sloppy, too confident and led him right to her? I sat there rethinking every time I spoke to Alita. She only called on the secret phone Serena and I used between ourselves. I'd made sure that every time Serena went to see her that Robert and his men were gone from the estate.

I'd been so sure we were being careful, but somehow he'd found her and he'd finally done what he'd threatened so often to do.

"You look upset, Ryder. Considering you never knew my wife, I have to assume your emotion is for me."

He knew damn well I'd cared for Alita. He knew I'd been the one to get her out of that house before Jesse arrived to do the job he'd been ordered to do by the very man who sat in front of me right now pretending to be upset over his wife's death. And he knew I'd helped Serena and the baby see Alita.

Pleased with how he'd taunted me, he said, "I need to tell my daughters about their mother's untimely passing."

"I think this news needs to come from me with Serena. Let me tell her."

"Hmmm…you might be right. Fine. You can be the one to tell her. I'll handle telling Janelle, and then I have to make the arrangements for the funeral."

He sounded like he was looking forward to that, like he used to when he gave those parties we all attended. My stomach turned at the thought of him playing the grieving husband in front of all his friends when he'd been the one who killed her.

I stood to leave as I struggled to keep my emotions hidden. I didn't want to give him the satisfaction of knowing how much what he'd done devastated me. He already seemed to be enjoying her death too much.

✦   ✦   ✦

STOPPING OUTSIDE THE NURSERY, I tried to think of how I would tell Serena her mother was gone. Jesus, I'd never had to say anything like this to anyone. She was going to be shattered when she heard, but I knew I had to be the one to tell her.

I opened the door a crack and saw her standing next to the baby's crib. After what I'd told her a few minutes before, she was already upset. How was I going to tell her this now?

She turned around and saw me, rushing into my arms and holding me tightly. Resting her head on my chest, she said, "I thought you were leaving. What was all that about, Ryder?"

I gently ran my hand over her hair and dreaded what I had to say. At the very least, I needed to get her away from Cayden when I broke the news.

"Let's go to our room, okay? We can talk there."

Serena tilted her head back and tried to smile. Wiping the tears from under her eyes, she nodded. "Okay. I just want to know why you said all those things."

Holding her hand, I walked back to our bedroom with her and prayed to God I'd find the right words to break this news to her. I remembered when the police had to tell me both my parents had been killed in that car crash. The old cop seemed more irritated than anything else that he had to be the one to tell me. He sat down in front of me and made a clucking noise like what he had to say disgusted him. Then he just blurted it out without any emotion or feeling.

I couldn't do that to Serena. Losing her mother again, this time forever, would be devastating. At the very least, she deserved to hear the horrible news from someone who cared how it would affect her.

She sat down on the bed and pulled her knees up to her chest, wrapping her arms around them like she always did when she was afraid. Watching me with wide eyes as I closed the door and walked toward her, she looked terrified to hear what I had to say.

If only I had to explain that I'd made a horrible mistake and thought the police were here for me.

I sat down and kissed her softly on the lips. "I'm sorry for before. I thought it was the police coming for me because of what happened in West Virginia. I didn't mean to upset you like that, Serena."

A sound like a whimper came out of her mouth, and she began to cry. "Oh, my God! But that didn't happen? I was so worried. What did my father want with you on your day off?"

Looking away, I searched for the right words but found none. "He had something he had to tell me."

"On your day off? He can't even give you that without bothering you about something?" she asked as she took hold of my hand.

I felt the tears begin to fill my eyes and willed them to go away, but it was no use. My heart broke for what I had to say.

"Ryder, what's wrong? Did my father do something?"

The word yes echoed in my brain. *Yes, he did something. He did what he'd threatened to do all this time. He killed her.*

I turned toward her and hung my head, not sure I knew how to tell her the mother she'd searched for and finally found was now gone. I looked up at her and saw the frightened look in her eyes again. I couldn't drag this out anymore. She had to know.

"Serena, I have something to tell you. I don't know how to say this."

"What is it? Are you hurt, Ryder?"

Shaking my head, I blew the air out of my lungs and realized I couldn't put it off any longer. "Alita and Michael were found dead this morning at their house. The police think it was a home invasion."

The words seemed to hang in the air between us, and Serena narrowed her eyes as her brain processed the news that her mother was dead. At first, she simply stared at me like she couldn't believe what I'd said, but then she began shaking her head back and forth quickly.

"No. No, that's not possible. I just talked to her last night. She's not...she's...she's fine. She's okay, Ryder. Tell me she's okay."

Pulling her into me, I held her tightly to me and said the words I knew I had to. "She's gone, Serena. I'm sorry."

Like the news took everything out of her, she slumped against me and began sobbing. "No! No, Ryder! Please tell me she isn't gone. Please! She can't be gone. She can't be."

"I'm sorry, Serena. I'm so sorry."

I held her as she cried like a baby, her body wracked with the total sadness that came from losing someone you loved. I wanted to fix this for her, to protect her from this, but I couldn't. All I could do was hold her in my arms as wave after wave of grief rolled over her.

"Please, tell me it's all a mistake," she sobbed into my shoulder. "Tell me they made a mistake. I can't go on without her, Ryder. It has to be a mistake."

"If I could tell you that, I would," I said quietly, stroking her back as she began to cry again. "I wish I could."

"After all the time I had to wait to find her, she's gone. She's really gone."

I wanted to say all the right things. To find a way to make her pain go away. But my sadness at losing Alita mixed with Serena's and the rage I wanted to hide from her about what Robert had done, so I sat there not saying anything.

Then when I thought she couldn't cry anymore, she sat back away from me and began to shake her head again. "I don't believe this was any home invasion like the police say it is. He did it. He finally did it. He killed her."

All I could do was nod in agreement. I had no real proof, but like Serena, I knew he did it. My gut said he finally crossed that line and took aim at the mother she'd missed all her life.

Serena stood from the bed and began pacing in

front of me. "I never thought he'd do it. You know that? I thought he used that threat as a bluff. That he just wanted to control me. And all along, he was just waiting for the moment when he would kill her. He finally found that moment, and now she's gone."

I reached out for her hand as she passed me, touching the tips of her fingers, but she yanked her hand away and kept walking. "He fucking did it. He took her away once and for all. It wasn't enough to make me grow up without a mother. No, he's a fucking monster. As soon as I found her, he probably began to plot out when it would hurt me the most to take her away again."

Standing from the bed, I stopped her and wrapped my arms around her. "Don't do this. He's not worth it."

Pushing me away, she looked up at me and twisted her face into a horrible grimace. Her eyes flashed a rage like I held inside me for him. "He actually said to me out in the garden the other day that it was a shame my mother wouldn't be around to see Cayden grow up. He knew what he was going to do even then, Ryder. He's a fucking monster who took away my mother and our son's grandmother. A monster!"

"Serena, we have to be careful now," I warned, unsure if I should even broach the subject that was on my mind.

"Why? He's already taken my mother from me. What else could he do?" she asked as she turned on her heels and began pacing again.

"If he's willing to go this far, then I don't know where he'll stop. I was afraid the police were here for me. He can make that happen any day he wants."

She stopped and spun around to face me, a look of horror in her eyes. "Why? Why take away everyone I love, Ryder? Is he just a monster, or is there something else behind this? What have I ever done to him to deserve this? All I wanted was to know my mother. To let her see that I grew up to be a normal woman and to share our son with her. Why was that so bad that he had to kill her?"

"I don't know. All I know is that he's worse than I ever imagined he could be."

Serena slowly walked toward me and took my hands in hers. "All I know is that I will never forgive him for this. I hate him. I wish he was dead."

As the words left her mouth, she broke down and fell to the bed sobbing. I held her once again, wishing I could do more and wondering if Robert had plans to get rid of me like he had Alita.

How far would his need to control Serena go?

Chapter Fourteen

Ryder

THE SUN SHINED like it was any ordinary day, but as we stood on the grass beside Alita's open grave, nothing felt like it would ever be the same again. For three days, Serena's emotions had swung like a pendulum back and forth between complete and utter sadness at the loss of her mother and unrelenting rage at her father for his part in taking her away forever this time.

Sometimes she cried for hours on end, unable to move from our bed where she lay curled up in a ball. Her devastation at Alita's passing crippled her unlike anything Robert had ever done before.

Then, as if possessed by a need to do something to feel some sense of power, she paced across the floor of our bedroom flailing her arms as she swore she'd never forgive her father for what he'd done and wishing him dead. When I stopped her by pulling her into my hold, she'd beat her fists against my chest, screaming for me to let her go, and then she'd collapse against my body, sobbing that she couldn't handle any of this.

And all the while, I held her and hated him for what he'd done. To her. To Alita and Michael. To us.

This morning, I wasn't even sure she'd be able to come to the funeral. The realization that today she'd say her final goodbyes to her mother set in right after she woke after sleeping for only an hour or so last night, more sleep than she'd gotten since I told her the news. She sat on the side of the bed and sobbed uncontrollably. She couldn't go to Cayden when he cried. She couldn't even stand.

She'd somehow found the strength to get herself dressed. Hiding beneath a large black hat, she sat next to me gripping my hand tightly, as if I was the only thing that kept her from running away from the horrible scene in front of us.

Next to me on the other side, Robert sat staring straight ahead listening to the minister eulogize his wife, his expression a void. The time for pretending had ended for him, but as I looked around at the people attending Alita's funeral, I saw many friends of his there to pay their respects.

He'd still pretend for them. He'd put on the grieving husband act and say all the words he knew would garner their sympathy. And if he could squeeze in some business while their hearts were open, all the better.

It's not like he'd cared about Alita. For fuck's

sake, he was the one who had her killed.

And for what? I had no idea. Because he could. Because it would show Serena and me that he had the power and we didn't.

Because he was a monster.

Beside Robert sat Janelle, who looked bored more than anything else as she stared off toward the cemetery's tree line. Who would expect more from her? I imagined Serena did, but not me. Janelle's look said she felt put out, not sad.

But maybe that was to be expected since she never knew her mother. Robert had made sure of that.

The minister finished speaking and approached Robert to express his sympathies for his loss once more. I watched, expecting him to flash one of his crocodile smiles, but he simply nodded and thanked the minister for his kind words.

He shook his hand and in a surprisingly humble tone, he said, "We all appreciate how wonderfully you spoke of my dearly departed wife, Reverend. You made a difficult time for all of us a tiny bit more bearable. Thank you."

The minister turned his attention to Janelle, who pretended like any of it mattered to her, and then Serena. She looked up at him, and the abject grief written all over her face appeared to surprise him for a moment. He opened his mouth and nothing came out.

Holding her hand, I tried to smooth over what had quickly become an awkward moment. "Thank you for everything, Reverend. I know Serena appreciates it."

Serena didn't react to my comment and simply continued to stare up at the man. He smiled at me and then touched her arm in a gesture of sympathy that all of a sudden made her break down and begin crying once again.

Robert quickly moved to escort the man away, as if Serena's genuine show of grief at the loss of her mother embarrassed him. Janelle stood looking down at us with an expression of confusion in her eyes. She had no idea why either of us should feel this much for someone who amounted to nearly a perfect stranger to her.

"Are you leaving now? I'd like to grab a ride back to the house with you two so I can get to see Cayden before I go home," she said with a cheeriness that sounded more appropriate to making plans to go out on a Friday night than a funeral.

Serena stared at the hole in the earth where her mother would find her final resting place and said nothing, so I answered, "I think it might be better if you go with your father, Janelle."

She shrugged and turned around to walk toward his car waiting on the road nearby. Robert had left the minister behind and stood talking to a group of men and women expressing their condolences. The whole scene felt surreal, like some kind of garden party at the estate with a casket and the hole it would be lowered into everyone found easy to ignore, except for Serena and me.

I turned to face her and the complete sadness she wore all over her face broke my heart. "Let's go. I think we should leave here."

She tore her gaze from the casket and looked blankly at me. "Okay."

We began walking to the car when I heard Robert yell, "Serena! Ryder! Come over here for a minute."

Horrified, I turned to see him standing with an older man and his wife, the three of them all smiles. I shook my head and kept walking with Serena toward the car, but he didn't let up.

"There are some people here I want you to meet."

Out of the corner of my eye, I saw Serena's expression twist into one of loathing at how her father had chosen to treat her mother's funeral like some chance to conduct business. I placed my hand on her back and tried to guide her away from him, but then I heard him say something I knew she could never let pass.

"My dear wife was troubled. Always had been.

I'd done all I could for her all these years to make sure she was comfortable, but now I can't help but regret not putting her in a facility where she would have been safe from a murderous home invasion."

Barely concealing his glee at Alita's death, he sounded glib and inappropriate. Serena heard what he said and something inside her snapped. Spinning on her heels, she stared at the small group of people with Robert at the center and balled her hands into fight fists.

"My mother wasn't sick or troubled! She was kind and good and deserved a life better than she got from you! Why don't you tell them what kind of husband you were, Daddy? Tell them where you sent her to, away from her own daughters and the life she should have had! Tell them or I will!"

Her outburst stunned everyone, especially Robert, and for a moment it felt like the world had stopped moving. I watched as his eyes grew wide for a split second before the crocodile smile appeared and then it faded as he seemed to remember where he was and how he was supposed to act.

Serena stood rigid at my side, ready for the fight she wanted, but I knew she wouldn't win so I pulled her away. "Come on. This isn't going to help. Let's go."

She stood staring bullet holes through him for another moment as he stared back at her in their emotional standoff that I sensed had only just begun. Tugging her arm, I turned her around and saw nothing but hatred in her face as she looked at me.

"I swear to God he's as guilty as the day is long, and someday he's going to pay for what he's done, Ryder."

"I know. Not today, but he will. I promise."

WE SLOWLY DROVE HOME without saying another word, and by the time we reached the house, Serena had slipped back into her grief. Hoping that seeing Cayden might help her to find some tiny bit of happiness, I took her to his nursery to let her sit with him for a while.

"I'm sure Cayden missed us while we were gone. It's the first time since he came home from the hospital that he hasn't been with you all day," I said as I opened the door to his room.

She smiled as we walked toward his crib. "I missed him too."

Happy to see her smile again, I looked down and saw Cayden wasn't in his bed. A look of fear settled into Serena's features, and she shook her head.

"Where is he? Why didn't Melanie put him down for a nap yet? This is when he should be in his crib for a nap."

"I'm sure she's on her way here right now. Let's go see where she is," I said, trying to comfort her.

But it didn't work. She ran out of the nursery and down the hallway to the stairs yelling, "Melanie! Where is Cayden? Melanie!"

By the time I caught up with her, she had made it to the kitchen to look for the maid we'd left in charge of Cayden while we attended the funeral. She should have been there waiting for us when we returned home, but she seemed to be nowhere to be found.

Serena spun around to face me, her eyes wide with fear. "Where is she? I told her to feed him and then put him down. Why wouldn't she be here or in his nursery, Ryder? Where could she be?"

"I'm sure she's just enjoying herself with him too much and forgot what time it was. Maybe she took him to her room."

My suggestion calmed her for the moment, and she took off like a shot toward the maid's quarters in the staff wing. I followed her, and when she broke into a run, I did too, catching up to her just outside the maid's door.

She banged on it, yelling, "Melanie! Open the door!"

The maid appeared a few seconds later looking confused by Serena's screaming. "Miss?"

"Where's Cayden? Why isn't he in his nursery?"

The maid shook her head. "Miss, I was going to put him down like you told me to, but Mr. Erickson came home and told me not to bother because he was taking him."

My blood ran cold as thoughts of Robert taking Cayden away from us filled my head. Serena grabbed my hand and squeezed it hard.

"Where did he take him, Melanie?" she asked in tears.

"I don't know, Miss. I didn't think… I just thought since he told me he was taking him and he's his grandfather that it would be okay."

Serena rushed off toward the main house, and I thanked Melanie for watching Cayden before running after her. I knew where she was going.

I hit the main hallway and heard her voice in Robert's study. She sounded frantic, and I knew I needed to get in there quickly.

"Give me Cayden, Daddy. He needs to be down for his nap."

"Relax. I'm just spending time with my grandson, Serena. It's a grandfather's prerogative."

Stopping as I stepped into Robert's office, I saw him standing in front of the bookcase with Cayden in his arms smiling like he always did when he was enjoying himself. I reached out to take Serena's hand, but she yanked her arm away and stepped toward them.

"Give me my son. Give him to me right now," she said, her voice becoming more frantic with each word.

But Robert merely waved her off and turned his attention to Cayden. "Your mommy wants to end our fun. We're not going to let her, now are we?" he said to him in that sugary sweet voice he used whenever he talked to the baby.

Serena took another step forward and put out her arms. "Give him to me, Daddy. Right now!"

"Robert, he needs to go down for a nap. Give him to Serena."

He didn't appear to even hear what I said. He simply stared at her as she stared back at him in their second standoff of the day. The room practically crackled with tension as they stood silently facing off, with only the occasional noise from Cayden.

Just as I thought he might do as I said, Serena screamed, "Give me my baby!"

I gently put my hand on her shoulder and tried to diffuse her anger. "Serena, he's okay. We'll put him down for a nap and you can sit with him all afternoon."

But it was no use. I'm not even sure she heard me.

"Give him to me now! I want him now!" she cried out in a desperate voice that sounded like a wounded animal's.

Robert looked stunned and then rattled by her outburst this time and handed Cayden to her without another word. Serena ran out of the room, leaving me standing there and wondering how much worse things could get before she snapped.

"My daughter seems to be taking her mother's death rather hard," he said in his usual relaxed tone as he walked behind his desk to sit down.

"Are you surprised? You know how much finding her mother meant to her. She's been asking you to help her for years."

"And she succeeded in that all on her own."

I knew asking him why he did it was probably a waste of breath, but I said, "So you knew. How did you find her?"

He smirked and shook his head. "I've known the whole time. What made you think you could hide that from me? Did you learn nothing in all your time here? Everyone works for me, Ryder. There are eyes everywhere, and they all watch for me."

"But why kill her? Nobody was being hurt, and Serena was happy to share the baby with her mother, something no one else, not even me, could give her."

My mention of Serena being happy made him frown, and he shook his head in disgust. "There are consequences to betrayal, Ryder. I would think you, of all people, would know that."

"She didn't betray anyone, Robert. She wanted to know her mother. That's not a betrayal of you. She was her mother, for Christ's sake. You took her away for what? To show you could? Do you want her to hate you?"

He winced for a moment and then sighed. "Her feelings for me have been the same for years. Long before you entered this house, she hated me. Someone had to pay for the betrayal. Perhaps now she'll learn her lesson."

"Be careful, Robert. The lesson you wanted to teach might not be the one she's learning."

I saw there was no point in talking to him anymore. Whatever he'd been before and whatever he'd done to me in the past, at least it hadn't been solely to intentionally hurt Serena. Now, all that had changed.

This monster didn't deserve my loyalty.

Chapter Fifteen

Serena

THE SOUND OF CAYDEN'S early morning crying came through the baby monitor telling me my time to sleep had ended, so I dragged myself out of bed and slowly walked down the hallway to his room to find him looking up at me with a smile I knew should have made my day.

But it didn't.

Nothing did anymore. It had been two weeks since my mother's funeral, and I still could barely bring myself to get out of bed. If it wasn't for Cayden, I wouldn't. I'd just stay under the covers and cry all day.

Nighttime was no better. I tried to sleep, but my thoughts wouldn't let me. I couldn't stop thinking about my mother and what she'd gone through all those years just to have it all mean nothing. She'd sworn to wait my father out, but in the end, he'd won and now she was gone.

She'd lived as a prisoner all those years, but she'd never given up. I loved that about her. I wanted to believe I could be that strong. Never knowing if she'd be free ever again, she still looked to the future and a time when she'd be reunited with Janelle and me again.

Now that would never happen for my sister. My father had made sure of that. Janelle would continue to think all the lies he told for our entire lives were the truth about our mother. I could try to convince her otherwise, but my father had done a very good job of making her the villain all those years.

To Janelle, our mother had abandoned us.

And what was the result of that? Janelle had grown up to be exactly what my father wanted in a daughter. Compliant. Shallow. Beautiful on the outside and empty on the inside. But she made a fine trophy for her husband. Just like my father thought women should be.

He'd never been able to convince me to be merely eye-candy for some man. I'd insisted on being someone on my own, much to his disappointment. I wanted to be strong. He wanted me to be like my sister.

Pliable. Easily manipulated by the promise of security and money. Subservient.

He'd been forced to imprison my mother to make her that, and he'd done his best to do the same to me. Maybe that was why he seemed to delight in torturing me. Because I reminded him of her.

The thought of that made me proud. I hoped I could be like her. I envied her strength and her ability to persevere. I only prayed to God I'd be able to now that she was gone.

I changed Cayden's diaper and sat down in the rocking chair with him in my arms to feed him as my mind went back to the few times I'd had with my mother in the past months. I knew I should cherish them, but all I felt was regret. If only I had told her more often how much I missed her all those years. If only I had said I love you more often.

If only.

Now there were no more chances to say any of those things to her.

Even worse, she would never get the chance to see her grandson grow up. She beamed happiness every minute she spent with him, and he loved her. She talked about what they'd do someday when things were different and she could go wherever she wanted to go. She'd take him to the zoo to see the animals and to the park to push him on the swings.

Those precious moments had been stolen from her when my father took her away the first time, and I had looked forward to Cayden getting to experience what I'd missed. Now he'd miss it too.

I looked down at his angelic face and my heart ached for all the wonderful things he'd never get to enjoy. He had a grandmother who loved him, and now all he had was a grandfather who was a monster.

Finished for the moment, Cayden looked up at me and smiled so innocently. He had no idea what he'd lost. He'd never get to know the woman who'd wanted so much to give him what she hadn't been able to give me.

It wasn't fair. None of it was fair. It shouldn't have been my mother and Michael taken away. It should have been my father.

Never before in my life had I wished my father dead. Not when he announced I couldn't go to school anymore and forced me to come home. Not when deep down I knew he lied every time he said he was looking for my mother but just couldn't find her. Not when he caught me with Ryder and sent me away for simply wanting to better myself by going to college. Not even when he forced me to marry a man I barely knew merely because it improved his bottom line.

None of those had made me hate him like I hated him now.

For so long, I'd dreamed of running away from this place so filled with everything in my father's world. To escape the ugliness that was so much a part of him. But then I found my mother, and for the briefest moment, I didn't hate living here with him. Having her in my life again made me feel like I could stand being around that world of his.

Without her, all my faith was gone. I couldn't survive here. Not with him.

And now as I sat hiding in my son's nursery, afraid at any minute my father might appear and force me to deal with him, I knew what had probably always been the truth.

Either he or I continued to exist. There was no other choice after what he'd done.

✧ ✧ ✧

WHEN I OPENED the door to the bedroom, I saw Ryder waiting for me. "How is our little guy doing this morning?" he asked in that kind voice I knew was his attempt to cheer me up.

I closed the door and sat down on the bed. "He's fine. I'm going to go back in with him after my shower."

The news that I didn't intend on spending most of my day in bed made Ryder's face light up. He crouched down in front of me and looked up with a genuinely happy expression I hadn't seen in weeks.

"That's great, Serena. I know he's missed you. I'm a poor substitute, I think."

I cupped my hand against his cheek and smiled. "You know that's not the truth. You're a great father, Ryder."

He leaned against my palm and returned the

smile. "I know, but I'm not his mother."

Looking down into his dark green eyes, I felt incredibly thankful I had such a wonderful man for a husband. Of all the things I'd been blessed with in this world, Ryder was the very best of all of them.

"I haven't been much of a mother for the past few weeks either. I know it's been hard dealing with me, but I want to thank you for being so patient. I just hope our son doesn't remember."

"All he's ever going to know is how much his mother loves him. And it wasn't hard dealing with you. It was just hard seeing you like that. I don't blame you, though, so if you're not ready to take care of Cayden yet, he's still got a father who can handle everything."

His gaze slowly traveled to my breasts and he smiled. "Well, almost everything."

Leave it to Ryder to make me giggle when I thought I couldn't. "You're silly, but I love you for trying to make me feel better."

"Nothing silly about it. Nature made women superior in that area."

I laughed again at how playful he could be, happy to finally have a reason to smile. "I'm happy to be able to feed our son. I just hope I start to feel good enough to do everything else I should be doing. In that area, I haven't been very superior."

Ryder slid his hands up my thighs and leaned

forward to kiss me. "You're always superior in that area. I don't blame you for not being in the mood. You lost someone you loved. You're supposed to be sad."

Shaking my head, I took a deep breath in as my emotions began to press on me. "I'm not sad. Not anymore. Now I'm angry."

He sat back on his haunches and a look of concern came over his face. "Anger is one of the steps toward acceptance. At least that's what they told me when I lost my parents."

"It's not that kind of anger. I accept that my mother is dead. What I don't accept is that the person responsible for her death still gets to walk around a free man. That I'll never accept as long as I live."

Drawing his eyebrows in, Ryder sighed. "I know, Serena. I know it doesn't seem fair, and it's not. It's not fair."

"I hate him. You know that? Hate him. Even after all he's done to me, I didn't hate him. I didn't understand why he seemed to love to torment me, but I didn't hate him. Not really. But now, I hate him with every fiber of my being."

"Serena…"

I cut him off before he tried to make me see how much hating my father could hurt me. I didn't care. The hate wasn't going anywhere as long as he and I co-existed in this world.

"Ryder, I know what you're going to say, but I can't. I can't stand to even see him. It's one of the reasons why I've stayed either in here or in Cayden's room since the funeral. I can't bear to run into him. I won't be able to keep the words I want to say from coming out. Hurtful, angry words. Words filled with the hate I feel for him."

"I know, but I don't want to see you get bitter because of him. He'll get his. I promise."

"I hate the thought of him walking around pretending to be the concerned husband when I know he did it. He had her killed. He had one of his men kill her. And all those friends of his standing around my mother's open grave as he lied through his teeth about the kind of person she was. He just stood there telling whoever would listen that he had tried to protect her. He's the one who had her killed. He might as well pulled the trigger and killed her himself."

Just hearing the words coming out of my mouth made me want to cry. My father had finally gone through with his threat and killed my mother.

Ryder hung his head. "I should have been more careful. I'm sorry. I don't know how, but somehow Robert found out where she was. I was so sure I was being careful. Maybe if I moved her, she might still be alive. I should have been more careful."

I ran my hand over the top of his head and leaned down to kiss him, loving the feel of his soft hair against my lips. "This isn't your fault, Ryder. I know you did everything you could to protect her and Michael. You didn't do this. You aren't to blame. He is."

"I know, but I can't help thinking if I'd only moved them he wouldn't have found her."

Cradling his head, I tilted it back so he looked at me. "You did everything you could. You saved her that night when Jesse came to kill her. You gave me more time with her."

His eyes filled with sadness. "I wish I could have saved her this time too so you could have longer with her."

"I know. You're not to blame for what happened. He is, and I hate him. I hate him so much that my body hurts sometimes when I think of how much I want him to suffer for what he did. It's like the hate is coursing through my veins now. I want nothing more than to see him pay for what he's done."

"About that..."

His expression morphed into one that looked like he had to break bad news to me. Hesitating, he finally said, "I have something I need to tell you."

Suddenly, I worried my father had done more than just kill my mother and her son. "What? Did my father do something? Tell me."

Kneeling in front of me, Ryder cleared his throat. "Do you remember that day of Cayden's doctor appointment when I didn't come in and you found me waiting outside?"

I'd expected him to say something terrible, so for a moment my brain scrambled to understand what he was talking about. "Yeah, I guess. His three month checkup, right? Why?"

"I didn't come in because I got stopped in the parking garage by two men from the FBI. They wanted me to turn on your father. I said I couldn't, and they didn't press it any further. But then the night I had to run to the store for diapers, they were there and that time they weren't willing to just make vague threats about what would happen if I didn't do what they want. They have something on me they say they're going to use if I don't help them get him."

He'd told me about the horrible things my father had him do when he worked for him, so I knew the FBI could have any number of ways to get Ryder. "What is it they have on you?" I asked, frightened to hear the answer.

Looking down, he avoided my gaze and answered, "What I did to that fighter in West Virginia. Of all the things I've done, they say they're going to use that."

My heart broke as he spoke the words. "So not

only have you been torturing yourself over that every night in your sleep, but now they want to make you pay for that if you don't turn on my father?"

Ryder lifted himself up so we were face to face. The sadness at what he'd done was etched into his expression. "I never meant to hurt him like that. I'd never hurt another fighter like I hurt him. I'd just wanted to earn enough money to get us away from here, but when it went bad, your father was the only one who could make sure I didn't go to jail. Now the FBI says they're going to make sure the authorities in West Virginia make me pay for what I did if I don't help them get your father."

He wrapped his arms around me and pressed his cheek to my body. I didn't blame Ryder for what happened. If my father hadn't made life here unbearable for me, he never would have wanted to make enough money to get me away from this place. As always, my father stood as the reason another person I loved was miserable.

Robert Erickson had done that one too many times. Now it was his time to suffer.

"Do it then. Help them. Give them what they want."

Ryder leaned back away from me and sat with his mouth agape and a look of shock on his face. "Do you know what you're saying? He'll go away for the rest of his life for what he's done, Serena. You have no idea what he's involved with."

"I know he's responsible for my mother's murder. He took her away, and now he has to pay."

"Can you live with me knowing I did this to him?"

"I can't live with knowing what he did to her, Ryder."

He nodded, and I knew what I'd just set into motion. I might not have known all the horrible things my father had done in his life, but I knew enough to be sure if the FBI made a case against him, he'd spend the rest of his life in prison.

Good. His life for the one he took. It wasn't an equal trade by any means, but it would have to do.

Chapter Sixteen

Ryder

EACH PERSON WHO noticed me as I sat in that out of the way coffee shop made my paranoia ratchet up another notch until by the time I'd sat there for fifteen minutes I was convinced every fucking person was there specifically to spy for Robert. Somewhere in my mind, I knew better since they barely gave me a passing glance before sitting down in their booths with their coffee and doughnuts, but that didn't change the fact that my nerves were practically frayed to their ends since I'd decided to do what the FBI wanted.

I kept my head down, staring at the red Formica tabletop and my cup of lukewarm coffee I hadn't drank much of. I felt like I stuck out like a sore thumb sitting there, like I had a big neon sign above my head that flashed I'M HERE WAITING TO MEET WITH THE FBI TO TURN ON MY BOSS.

"Keep your cool, Ryder," I whispered under my breath as another person walked through the front door. "Don't let your paranoia get the best of you."

They were supposed to show up in the parking lot within the next five minutes and I would get in their car to meet with them. I'd repeated the plan a hundred times in my head to convince myself that I wouldn't be caught and disappear before the night ended, gone from Serena and Cayden forever without even a goodbye. And every time I reminded myself that I was doing this for them.

She deserved to live without the fear that at any time Robert would make me disappear or take Cayden from her. No one should have to go through life like that.

Night after night as I lay in bed too terrified by my nightmares to go back to sleep, I thought about what our life would be like once we were free. Before Cayden came along, I used to have a fantasy of Serena and me going wherever our hearts took us. We could live in the mountains in that cabin I knew like the back of my hand with its grey stone fireplace in the living room where we would sit as I held her in my arms and we enjoyed the peace of being just the two of us finally. We'd talk about what the future might hold for us, all the while loving how we could choose to come and go as we pleased.

Once Cayden was born, that dream of what we'd do after we escaped Robert and the ugliness of his world changed. Gone were the ideas of us traveling wherever we wanted to because we could. A baby made that kind of bohemian life impossible.

But even though the idea of what we'd be changed, the feeling still remained. Now we'd just be three free souls instead of two.

I wanted to give Serena and Cayden that. They deserved it, and if that meant I had to work with the FBI, then the risk was nothing I couldn't handle.

Except at the moment as I waited to see the agents pull into the parking lot and my mind spun out of control that at any minute I'd be made, I wasn't handling things all too fucking well. Wiping beads of sweat off my brow even as an old air conditioning unit blew ice cold air out directly toward where I sat, I stared out the plate glass window at the front of the coffee shop and told myself this was going to be all right.

I saw them drive into the lot and park in a spot farthest away from the building. My heart began slamming against my ribcage as I realized this was actually happening. I was going to tell them everything Robert had done. I was going to turn on the man who had called me his adopted son for nearly three years.

The man who had given me a roof over my head and a life better than living in that cinder block room in the warehouse.

The man who had commanded his men to beat me senseless because I had done what he should have to Oliver for trying to kill Serena.

The man who would someday give the order to kill me.

I watched the red brake lights on the black sedan flash twice to give me the signal to come out and stood up from the booth. My knees buckled, sending me lurching forward until I caught my balance.

Stay calm. You can do this. You have to do this.

Sure someone would notice me getting into a strange car, I hurried over to the back door and quickly slipped inside. Pressing my back against the seat, I took a deep breath and let it out slowly, happy that at least I had made it this far.

The guy who almost never spoke turned around in the driver seat to look at me. "You okay? We haven't even gotten to the hard part yet and you look like you're going to pass out."

From the first time I saw these two, I didn't like this guy. Something about his hair and the way it looked like some barber had mowed it like a lawn close to his head to create a flat top made him look like a hard ass. He only spoke to me once before this, but he always seemed to be scowling at me.

I didn't need his judgment. He could fuck off if that's what he thought he'd be giving me. I knew what I'd done, and I still wouldn't be taking any of his opinions on my fucking life.

"I'm fine. Fuck, I've gone round after round with

behemoths in the ring. I think I can handle sitting at a fucking coffee shop waiting for you two."

The one who usually did the speaking turned around in the passenger seat and smiled as if he was having a good time. Now that I looked at him, I noticed he had that same asshole hairstyle as his partner, but it didn't make him seem like the hard ass it did the other guy. Plus, even though he had never been what I'd call friendly, I had a sense he wasn't judging anyone so much as pulling no punches when he spoke to me.

"You ready?"

Nodding, I took another deep breath in and let it out slowly. I was ready. I didn't have a choice anymore. I had to be ready.

"Yeah. Let's do this."

"We're going to need you to wear a wire. You understand that, right?"

A chill ran up my spine. How many movies had I seen where the damn guy wearing a wire made it out alive in the end? Not too fucking many.

These two guys didn't need to know how unbelievably fucking terrified wearing a wire made me. I'd heard Robert threaten to chop people up if he thought they were recording him on a business call, and he never had any proof that they were doing anything wrong. A wire taped to my body was a hell of a lot more evidence of my guilt.

"If that's what it takes," I said flatly, trying to sound far more casual than I actually felt about the whole thing.

"Good. Well, let's get started," the guy in the passenger seat said with a smile.

But I wasn't ready to get things going just yet. I needed some details settled before I did anything.

Holding my hand up, I stopped him before he began rattling off orders. "Hang on. I need to know a few things before we start."

The two of them looked at each other with a knowing expression and then looked back at me. The guy in the passenger seat pursed his lips and nodded. "Okay. Shoot."

"I need to know whatever happens Serena and Cayden are kept out of it. She knows nothing about what her father has done. I don't want them hurt in any of this."

"Fine. But you need to tell us exactly what he's done and you're going to have to get him to talk about it while you're bugged up. Give us both of those things and you've got immunity."

"I'll do as much as I can. I can't promise he's going to act like it's true confession time just because I'm sitting in front of him."

"Well, you better hope he does. Your job is to get him on the record, and the more times you're wired up, the harder it gets."

None of this was making me feel any better, but I didn't want these two to know that. Shrugging, I nodded. "I got it. It's not rocket science. Get him to talk so you get him admitting what he did."

They seemed fooled by the matter-of-fact way I said that, so the guy in the passenger seat went back to asking about what Robert had done like they didn't already know. The truth was, though, they probably only knew a fraction of what he'd done.

But they'd know now.

I pointed at the guy in the driver's seat. "You better get a pen and paper out. You're going to need to write this stuff down. There's a lot."

He didn't say anything back to me, surprisingly, and did as I told him to. When he was ready, I cleared my throat and began telling them everything I'd seen in the years I worked for Robert.

I'd kept the laundry list of things in my head, unable to forget some of them while struggling to remember the finer details of many of the things he'd ordered us to do to those who crossed him. I figured I'd start small and build up to the bigger crimes he'd committed.

"Well, I'm assuming you know about the strip club. The Red Velvet Room. That's never been completely legal, but since the local cops never seemed to care much about it, I assume it's not really on your radar either. But the drug dealing might be."

Passenger seat guy nodded. "We know about the drug trade going through there. Is Erickson in charge of that? I can't see a guy like him getting involved in heroin dealing."

I laughed at his assumption that Robert was too fancy to be involved with anything illegal. "He's in charge of everything that happens around him. If he didn't directly benefit from the sale of that shit in his club, it wouldn't happen in his club. Period. He's the one who arranges the whole damn thing. The bouncer there, a guy named Chris Blandon, is the one who handles it for Robert, but he's just the lackey compared to his boss."

"How much are we talking here?" FBI guy in the passenger seat asked as the other one wrote down the details.

Shaking my head, I shrugged. "That I don't know. I was never part of that, but I knew it was going on. One of the dancers told me she saw it happening."

"What's her name?"

"Kitty Cerra."

The two of them looked at each other and smiled. "Your ex-girlfriend. Got it," the driver said with a chuckle.

I let the crack about Kitty slide and continued telling them what I knew. "He's also branched out into prostitution with some of the dancers, and I overheard things about some of them being there because of some deal he made with some Russian."

Both the men looked into the backseat, and I knew I'd said something new to them by the way their eyes opened wide.

"Are you saying human trafficking? Erickson's involved in human trafficking?"

"I don't know, but I overheard him talking to the guy who runs the club for him about two Russian girls who just appeared one day about six months ago."

The driver seat guy wrote feverishly as I spoke, and I knew this was something they hadn't figured out on their own yet.

"Keep going," the passenger seat guy said. "Is there more?"

"You know about the underground fights, I'm sure. That alone makes him millions, but again, the local boys don't seem interested enough to give him a hard time anymore. Hell, the last few times I fought at The Pit, they had intro music blaring. When I met him, it was way more hush hush. I guess he found a way to convince the Baltimore cops to look the other way."

"Who's in charge of the fighting, Erickson or someone else?"

"There's no one else in charge of anything. I think you guys have the wrong idea about him. He controls everything. The people around him, what they do, how things turn out. All of it is controlled by him."

"Well, he doesn't go out and find the fighters, does he? Did he have you do that once you began working for him?"

I shook my head, hating that I had to bring Floyd's name into this. He didn't deserve to be dragged down with Robert.

"No, I never did that for him. He's got a guy who runs the fights and handles the money they bring in."

"Well, what's his name?" the driver seat guy asked, impatient with my reluctance to say the name.

"He only works for him like I do. Does he really have to be involved in this?"

The passenger seat guy held up his hand. "We're not out to get the minor players here, but we need to know the names to get them to talk too."

"Floyd. Floyd Marcinko."

"And with these fights, does this Floyd run the gambling that goes along with them?"

I nodded, not wanting to indict Floyd any more than I already had. "Yeah, but it's all Robert. Floyd just does the dirty work. Robert is the one who takes it all. Floyd doesn't get anything from the gambling. He just gets paid to be a trainer for the fighters."

They looked suspicious, like my defending Floyd

was wrong, but I didn't care. Floyd wasn't a villain in all this. He did right by us fighters any time he could, and he'd saved my ass more than once.

I ran through the list of things I knew Robert had done. The drugs at the club. The Russian girls. Prostitution. The underground fighting and the gambling that went with it. There was only one more.

The people he'd had killed.

Swallowing hard, knowing I had been the one who had killed some of them, I said, "I can tell you the names of the people he's had taken care of that I know of. Some are people I've done myself, and others were someone else's job."

The passenger seat guy winced at my explanation and nodded. "Okay. Start with the ones you were personally involved with. Then we can go from there."

I took a deep breath in and held it inside my lungs for a long moment. What I said now would be enough to put me away for the rest of my life. I knew the chance I was taking telling these guys about what I'd done, but I didn't have a choice anymore. When Robert killed Alita, he stepped over the line. I knew it would be just a matter of time before he came for me, or even worse, Serena.

Blowing the air out, I decided which name I'd start with. One of them I couldn't seem to shake the memory of even now.

"Jacob Landon. He ordered me to kill him because of something he said about his daughter. I drowned him in his hot tub."

The sound of the words didn't reflect any of the emotions I attached to what I'd done. I only needed to give the pertinent information. They didn't care what I felt about each one.

"Your wife's former brother-in-law," driver seat guy said, as if that information was important to the fact that I'd killed Jacob on Robert's command.

I nodded and continued with the next name. "George Ingram. He ordered his death because he cheated him on a deal. I don't know any more than that. He was right after I started working for him as security."

Without lifting his head, driver seat guy asked, "How did you do it?"

"Two to the head with a .38," I answered honestly, my mouth suddenly dry.

He scribbled down my answer and looked up. "Okay. Keep going."

"There's only one more that he had me do. Jasper Krieg. I don't know what he did to him. All I know is that he was part of a group of guys who used to be at the Red Velvet Room all the time."

I stopped for a moment as I remembered the night I found him drunk in his car behind the club.

Barely alive after all the booze he'd poured down his throat that night, he was the easiest of them all to do.

"And I smothered him with a jacket from his back seat as he sat in his car."

The passenger seat guy raised his eyebrows in surprise. "You're not exactly the usual kind of hit man. Most have a trademark style. Why don't you?"

Leaning forward, I pointed my finger at him. "I'm not a fucking hit man. I was a fighter Robert Erickson bought, and when I pissed him off by falling in love with one of his daughters, he had me beaten so I couldn't fight anymore. When he offered me a job as security on his estate, I took it because I was fucking homeless and figured I could be some wealthy guy's hired help. I didn't realize security to him meant something else, and by the time he had me doing these three, I was in too deep. So no, I'm not a hit man and I don't have a style. I might not have cried a bucket full of tears when I took care of these people or when I had to rough up the others, but I never wanted to kill anyone."

"And Oliver Landon? Did he order you to kill him for what he did to Serena?"

I sat back hard against the seat and shook my head. There was no point in turning back. Now I'd see if that promise of immunity was any good.

"No. He didn't order that."

"You did that on your own?"

Looking out the car window at the yellow coffee shop sign as it flickered in the dark, I couldn't say I felt any guilt at that moment for what I'd done to Oliver. The others? Yeah. I hated what I'd done to them, but not to Oliver. Not after what he did to her.

I turned back to face the two men in the seat in front of me and saw them waiting for my answer. There was only one truth I knew. It's all I'd ever known since that night I saw Serena standing outside my bedroom door.

"Whatever I've done, all I wanted to do was keep Serena safe. Whatever loyalty I've shown to Robert Erickson, it was all to protect her."

The car fell silent for a few moments until the driver asked, "Is there anything else?"

I thought about his question for a moment and answered, "Nothing you wouldn't know more about than I do. He's close to a few politicians, so you know they have to be in his pocket. And the cops are the same."

"We know all about that."

Quietly, I said, "And Jesse, but the cops decided not to charge me for that because I was protecting Serena."

"Yeah, that's not part of this. But now we just need you to get him to talk about all of it."

Back to the wire. I dreaded the very idea of walking into Robert's office wearing that damn thing, but I knew it had to be done.

"Yeah. I know. I'll do it."

As the driver slipped the pen and paper into his suit coat, the passenger reached back and patted me on the arm. "You did good. Now all you have to do is get him to talk to you. He thinks of you as a son, so that shouldn't be too hard, right?"

I smiled, but inside I wondered just how much Robert thought of me as his son these days.

Chapter Seventeen

Serena

A WARM BREEZE blew as I walked down the narrow paved road with Cayden in my arms, his little baseball cap pulled down low on his face so the midday sun wouldn't burn his tender skin. I lifted it slightly to see his eyes, and he smiled up at me, not knowing where we were going was no place for happiness.

My mother's final resting place sat in the middle of a long row of graves at Cathedral Cemetery. My father spent a small fortune on the expensive marble memorial that looked awkward surrounded by more modest headstones. Why I had no idea. There was something truly perverse about spending thousands of dollars on someone you hated enough to kill.

Or maybe he did it as a celebration of his success in finally getting rid of her. Sort of a monument to himself and his evil heart.

I didn't want to constantly be so full of hate. I didn't. I felt it beginning to consume even the best parts of me. But no matter how hard I tried, I couldn't push past it every time I thought about how much I wanted to tell my mother all about what Cayden was up to or that I hoped I was pregnant again and couldn't wait to find out so I could tell Ryder.

All of those wonderful things she'd never get to hear about. She'd never get to see Cayden walk or talk. Or his first day of kindergarten. And if I was pregnant, she'd never get to meet him or her.

For all of that and more, I hated my father with every part of me. And every day that hatred grew.

Cayden fussed in my hold, so I switched him to the other arm, juggling the pot of flowers in my hand, and tickled his nose with mine. "We're almost there, little man. Patience, grasshopper."

He made a noise that told me his patience was quickly growing thin with this walk and all the jostling around I was doing to him. I should have brought the stroller, but it was bad enough that I had to let that ridiculous goon of my father's come with us.

I looked back toward the car and sneered in disgust at the man who stood outside the car with his arms folded over his chest looking bored. As if he had anything better to do. If he wasn't waiting for us while we visited my mother's grave, he'd be back at his post holding up the bookcase in my father's office.

He could stand out in the sun in that dark suit of his for as long as I chose to spend with my mother. I didn't care if he melted into the pavement. All the better. Then I wouldn't have to drive home next to his creepy self looking over at me every two minutes like he had orders to study if I was up to something my father should know about and report back in detail to him.

I saw my mother's grave and stepped onto the grass to walk the two rows in. Even in the eighty degree temperatures of the late August day, it still felt cool against my toes as it brushed the outside of my sandals. Kneeling down in front of her memorial, I placed Cayden in the grass and the flowers at my side as I read the inscription my father had put on the marble.

Alita Erickson, dear wife and loving mother, taken from us all too soon.

If there was such a thing as a hateful eye roll, I did it while I gritted my teeth in anger. Taken from us all too soon was right. My mother practically cried out for justice from the grave through those words.

I ran my fingertips over the letters etched in the stone and whispered, "I promise you, Mom, he won't go unpunished. If it's the last thing I do in this world, I'll make sure of that."

Tears welled in my eyes, and I let them flow as I

sat there sharing time with my mother the only way I could now. Cayden played beside me, giggling as he tightened his chubby little fists around a tuft of grass and pulled as hard as he could only to have it slip through his hands. I knew it was stupid, but I hoped she heard his laughter and got to share in it somehow.

"The baby's here with me, Mom. You should see him. He's growing like a weed. The clothes I had for him even a month ago are too small on him now. Ryder says he's going to be a big boy because his hands are so big. Like baseball mitts."

I stopped and looked over at Cayden. Rubbing his belly, I tickled him for a second and he giggled in that way that never failed to make me smile.

"Hear that? He's such a happy baby, Mom. Do you remember that time when you had him in your arms and you were singing to him? He loved that so much. I try to sing to him sometimes, but I don't have a beautiful voice like yours."

The words caught in my throat, and I had to stop before the tears came again. I didn't want to spend my whole time there crying. Yes, she was gone, but I knew I needed to come to that place of acceptance Ryder talked about.

Even if it felt wrong to finally admit that. No private detective could find her this time. She was gone forever.

Wiping my eyes, I smiled down at Cayden and continued talking, feeling some kind of relief as I did. "So Mom, I have news to tell you. I don't know yet, but I might be pregnant again. I won't know for a week or so, but it feels like it did when I was first carrying Cayden. Isn't that great? He might have a baby brother or sister by this time next year."

I instinctively waited for an answer, even though none could ever come. I wanted to believe somewhere she was hearing me and happy for us. It was foolish and maybe even childish, but I liked to imagine her as my guardian angel, and when I came to sit at her grave and talk to her, I hoped she knew I was there to share my life with her.

Cayden grew sleepy, so I planted the white daisies across the front of the memorial and stepped back to look at them. They were so much less than she deserved, but I hoped they gave anyone who saw them a hint about the kind of person she'd been.

Cheerful. Kind. A loving soul. A good soul.

"I'm sorry you won't get to be there as your grandson grows up, Mom. You deserved so much better than you got. I won't ever forget you and how much you showed me about strength and goodness. I hope you know what finding you meant to me. I hope I make you proud."

With tears in my eyes, I picked up the baby and began walking back to the car where my father's goon stood waiting. I didn't speak to him as I fastened Cayden in his car seat and started the car before he even got in.

That's how much I cared about him and the man he worked for. I'd happily leave them all behind in a cemetery.

CAYDEN CRIED THE entire way home—all thirty-five minutes—and I secretly enjoyed how miserable that made the man sitting in the passenger seat. Out of the corner of my eye, I saw him wince more than once when the baby hit one of those particularly screechy notes he often could when he was irritable. By the time we pulled onto the estate, I had a feeling he was as miserable as my son.

Good. Couldn't happen to a nicer guy.

As soon as the car stopped, he jumped out and marched away inside the house. I imagined he would give my father the rundown of what I'd been up to when I ventured out into the world, careful to not elaborate on how cranky his grandson had been on the drive home so he didn't offend his boss.

Cayden's crying ceased the minute I took him out of the car seat, and as we walked through the main hallway, I whispered in his ear, "That's Mommy's little boy. What do you say we go upstairs and have something to eat?"

Just as I passed my father's office, I heard him

yell out, "Serena, I want to speak to you!"

I pulled the baby close and took a deep breath in, trying not to let my emotions get the best of me. Without even looking in, I kept walking toward the stairs and said, "Cayden needs to be fed. I can come down after he goes down for the night."

"Serena, I want to speak to you now," he answered in a voice bristling with anger.

Stopping, I quietly promised Cayden someday we wouldn't have to live like this and turned around to head into my father's office to listen to whatever nonsense he had to tell me. He sat behind his desk like usual, but the look on his face indicated he was perfectly pleased with something. I dreaded finding out what.

"I really need to take care of the baby, so can we make this quick?" I asked as I stopped just inside the doorway.

"How was your day out?"

"Fine. I think your man had a particularly good time, courtesy of my son," I answered, happy to make someone as miserable about my father's ridiculous rule as it made me.

"Really? I'll have to ask Harden," he said, clearly not understanding the sarcasm dripping off every word out of my mouth.

"Is that all you wanted?" I asked, turning to leave.

"Not quite. Before you go, I wanted to let you know I'll be having someone move into my townhouse."

Bile rose into my throat at how disgusted he made me. "Tired of pretending to be the grieving husband, Dad? I guess it's unnecessary anyway. Everyone here knows the truth."

His smile faded a bit, but not enough to turn into a frown. Instead, he narrowed his eyes at my accusation for just the briefest moment and then simply moved on.

"I didn't want you to be surprised when you ran into her in the kitchen one night."

"Why would I run into anyone here, Dad? She isn't going to be living in this house, is she?" I asked, sickened by this discussion.

He extended his arm, and I followed where it pointed toward the back of his office. Before my mind registered who was standing there, the sickening sweet smell of that cheap perfume hit my nose as she stepped toward him to take his hand.

Kitty.

Her too-tight red dress showed far more cleavage than I wanted anywhere near my child, and I worried her boobs would pop out of it at any moment. God, she was awful with her stringy blond hair and garish makeup that made her look like she'd just stepped off stage.

So that was what strippers wore when they wanted to make a good impression on their new neighbors. I couldn't imagine what she'd dress herself in if she wanted to borrow a cup of sugar.

"You remember Kitty, don't you? She's been a shoulder for me to cry on in these past weeks, which have been so trying."

"How nice. I'm sure she's been so much more than that."

"She'll be moving onto the estate today. I'm sure you and Ryder will make her feel welcome."

When he said Ryder's name, his mouth turned up into one of those crocodile smiles I hated. The thought of this stripper living in the same place as us sickened me. This was my house. I'd lived here all my life. I'd suffered through every indignity my father had forced on me here, and now I'd have to tolerate this woman moving in like some cut-rate replacement for my mother.

Even worse, she was the ex of the man I loved and the father of my child. This was just another nasty ploy of my father's to control me and try to drive a wedge between Ryder and me.

And I had no intention of taking the bait. At least not in front of him.

I sneered at her as she wound her arm around my father's. "So now we have former strippers living on the estate? Or is she still taking off her clothes for men in exchange for money?"

She snapped, "I haven't done that in months, for your information."

Looking her up and down, I'd seen more than enough and turned my attention back to my father. "How nice."

"You know, Ryder never held my career against me."

I glanced over at her and saw her wearing a smug expression I wanted to smack right off her face. How dare she bring up her past with him?

Before I could say what I thought of her so-called career and put her in her place, my father cut me off. "You never held Ryder's past as a fighter against him. I'm sure you can do the same for Kitty."

That my father thought comparing Ryder's past with this woman's was anything acceptable infuriated me, and before I said something that would let both of them know how much this new arrangement upset me, I turned on my heels and left the office. I wanted to scream, but thankfully, having Cayden in my arms kept me from yelling at the top of my lungs what I wanted to do for dear Kitty.

By the time I reached the nursery, I was muttering under my breath, "I'm not supposed to hold her past against her? Who does he think he is? What makes him think it's okay to bring that woman into this house?"

I sat down in the rocking chair and unbuttoned my blouse so Cayden could feed while my blood nearly boiled about what I'd just heard. My father had done some underhanded things to me in the past, but bringing Ryder's ex to live just a few yards away from me was beyond the pale.

As I sat there hiding in my son's room like I so often did lately, Ryder came in all smiles to see us. "How are my two favorite people today?"

"My father is moving in your ex-girlfriend today. That's how this favorite person is doing."

He stopped dead and opened his mouth to speak, but nothing came out. Finally, he said, "My ex-girlfriend?"

"Kitty," I answered, practically spitting her name out like a bite of rancid food.

Still confused, he shook his head like what I said couldn't be what I meant. "Why? What would he bring her here for?"

"They're together, so now that his period of mourning is over, he's moving her in to his townhouse. I expect we're all going to be enjoying Sunday brunch on the patio this weekend."

Cayden finished eating and I readied him for a nap, but I could barely contain my anger over our new houseguest. Ryder took him into his arms to play for a little while, but I was in no mood for playtime. I kissed him on the forehead and tickled his nose with mine, like I did every time before I put him into his crib.

"Sleep tight, Cayden. Sweet dreams."

I turned to leave, but Ryder caught me by the arm. "Serena, don't go. We need to talk about this."

"Talk about what? I'm angry, and I don't want to be like that in my son's nursery, so I'm going to our room and when you and he are done, I'll be there. Then we can talk."

The look on his face as I walked away told me he wasn't any happier with having Kitty at the house than I was, but that did little to soothe my anger about the whole situation. I left him to play with our son and walked to our bedroom, fighting the urge to march right downstairs and give my father a piece of my mind about his new girlfriend and these new living arrangements.

I couldn't do that, though. Then he'd know how much it bothered me and he'd have won. It wasn't much of a battle, for sure, but each one with him was worth the fight. Let him think I didn't care about his little stunt to cause problems between Ryder and me.

Every minute that passed made me seethe even more, so by the time Ryder came to the room nearly a half hour later, I had to curb my urge to lash out at him and not do exactly what my father hoped I would.

He stopped me as I paced away from the door,

wrapping his arms around my waist and nuzzling my neck. "She won't be here for long. Once he's gone, she'll be gone too."

"I don't care how long she's here. I hate it. Do you know what it's like to know you were with her and now she's here in my house?" I asked as I tried to remain angry with his arms tenderly holding me to him.

"He's doing this to control us, Serena. Don't let him. She means nothing to me," he said softly in my ear.

Turning in his hold, I looked into his eyes and saw the truth. She didn't mean anything to him. I knew that. It was just the fact that she had been with him, even before I had. She knew him in a way I did, and I hated the idea of sharing that with her.

"I can't live like this, Ryder. He's taunting me. Taunting us. He wants us to know he holds all the cards, and he'll play them as he sees fit. He's going to make sure you and she are put together as often as possible. I know him. This is some ploy to drive us apart."

"Nothing he can do can change that I love you and you love me. I'm your husband, and you're my wife, Serena. It doesn't matter who he moves in. His time is nearly over."

I knew what he meant and I wouldn't shed a single tear when my father got what was coming to him courtesy of the FBI. "When?"

"Tonight. It's all set."

"Your eyes tell me you're not sure. Have you changed your mind?"

Ryder shook his head and then kissed me softly on the lips, lingering there a minute before he said, "I know what has to be done. I haven't changed my mind."

"I love you. No matter what he tries, that won't change, Ryder."

He pressed his forehead to mine and smiled. "Good, because I plan on sticking around for the rest of my life, and I plan on that life being good and long."

As he held me in his arms, I closed my eyes and exhaled, safe no matter what madness my father tried to force on us. His world was about to close in on him. His days of tormenting everyone around him were numbered.

"I want you to stay safe, okay?" I whispered into Ryder's shoulder. "You've got too much to live for."

Tilting my head back, he smiled. "I do. I've got the best wife in the world and a beautiful son she gave me. What else could a man ask for?"

Even though I didn't know for sure if I was pregnant or not, I pressed a kiss onto his lips and answered his question. "A second son or maybe a daughter?"

For a moment, he just stared down into my eyes, like he was searching for the meaning of what I'd said, but then his eyes lit up with understanding. "Are you?"

"I don't know. I probably shouldn't have said anything until I do, but I wanted to make sure you knew you have a family that needs you. No matter what the FBI wants, we want to spend a lifetime with you."

His hands slid down over my belly and rested there. "Whether you are or not, I still have everything to live for. Don't worry. I'm not planning on doing anything stupid. I'll just get them what they want and then it'll be over."

"Will it finally be over?"

I wanted to believe him when he said that. I wanted to believe more than I'd ever believed in anything before that it would all be over soon and we'd be free.

"It will. I just need you to trust me," he said sweetly.

As if I had a choice. I loved him too much to do anything else.

Chapter Eighteen

Ryder

I STOOD OUTSIDE ROBERT'S office, my heart racing, and took a deep breath before I set into motion events that I'd have no control over once I stepped into that room. There was no turning back now. The second he let me in would be the one that signaled the end for him.

Before I could even raise my hand to knock, he called out to me. "Taken to lurking outside doorways? You've been spending too much time around my daughter. Come in, Ryder."

I couldn't help but smile as I walked in and stopped near the doorway. "I just wanted to see if you had some time to talk."

"Of course. Take a seat," he said, gesturing toward the red leather chairs in front of his desk.

Looking around the room, I saw two of his men in front of the bookcase and one standing near the window further down the wall. They needed to go for this to work.

I turned back to face him. "Privately."

Robert cocked one eyebrow and grinned one of his crocodile smiles. "You remember being one of my men, Ryder. You can talk freely in front of them."

"It's about Serena. I don't want to talk in front of others about your daughter. I'm sure you don't either."

For a moment, he looked like he might give me an argument about that, but then he simply shrugged and waved the men out of the room. They filed out as his men always did—silently and quickly—so in no time it was just the two of us.

"So now will you sit, Ryder? Or are we that formal these days that you can't even sit down with me anymore?"

I sat down and worked to look as calm as I should, even as my heart was pounding like a jackhammer against my chest. Scrambling to think of what to say, I was surprised when he began talking first.

"Now that we're alone, what would you like to talk about concerning Serena?"

Best to start with something that could get him talking, so I went in for the kill. "Serena is having a hard time dealing with Kitty living here now. I'm sure you can understand why."

Again, he arched his eyebrow. "Because you used to fuck her?"

At my sides, I curled my hands into fists. We were sitting there talking about how his own daughter wasn't comfortable with him bringing one of my exes to the house to live, and he had to act like that.

Like a fucking pig.

"She was a stripper who worked for you. Still does, I think. Right? We all worked for you doing some pretty terrible things."

Ignoring my comment about Kitty's still dancing for him at the Red Velvet Room, he stood up and walked over to the bar. "Terrible things. Interesting. So now you have a conscience, son? After all you've done for me, now you think it was terrible? That's my daughter's influence, no doubt. Serena always did have a strange sense of propriety."

Staring straight ahead, I worked to keep focused, even as I wanted to take a much-deserved shot at him. "Having a child brought things into focus, I guess. I did what I did then, but I don't think I could do that now."

I listened as he dropped one and then two ice cubes into his glass before pouring the bourbon and branch water into it. A quick swirl of them all and he turned around to walk back to his desk, but instead stopped next to where I sat.

"Like killing all those people? Like Oliver, who you did all on your own? Or beating up all those men, again some who you did all on your own like that poor fuck up in West Virginia? Terrible indeed. It would be terrible if you had to answer for that horrible mistake you made with him, wouldn't it, Ryder?"

"Underground fighting sometimes gets ugly. You'd know that better than anyone else," I answered flatly, sure he could hear my heart pounding as he hovered next to me.

He was playing with me. I didn't know if he suspected me of turning on him, but something was different with him now. Something about the way he saw me.

"Are we going to take a walk down memory lane, son?" he said in a low voice, sending chills down my spine.

I turned my head and looked up at him to see him watching me carefully. He wanted to unnerve me.

The problem was he was succeeding and doing a damn good job at it. If he realized I was wearing a wire, he'd kill me. Of that, I was sure.

"If that's what you want, Robert," I answered, my gaze never wavering from his.

A slow smile spread across his face, and he slapped me on the back. "You're a ballsy son of a bitch, son. A cocky, ballsy son of a bitch. Always have been since the first time I met you. No matter what, I appreciate that. It's that kind of attitude that helps a man make it in this world."

I knew what he meant, and before Serena and Cayden, I would have agreed. In the ring, being cocky often meant the difference between getting my hand raised at the end of the match and limping away bloody and beaten. But now that I had a family to care for and the possibility of another child coming soon, I didn't want to be a cocky fuck anymore.

At least not the kind Robert admired.

"I'm just a father nowadays. I spend my days watching monitors for you and listening to Johnson talk about fish and my nights with Serena and Cayden. He doesn't care if I'm cocky or not."

Robert returned to his seat and shook his head. "Sounds like you're going soft, son. Are you really going to be happy just doing that for the rest of your life? Working all day at some boring job and playing house at night? I don't think that's who you are."

I had to bite my tongue because I wanted to tell him he had no fucking idea about who I really was. He'd created this person he'd wanted me to be before he ever met me. He wanted a son who followed in his footsteps and did what he'd never done.

But I wasn't that person. I'd never been him. I was just some fighter he found and brought home who fell hard for a girl. Everything else was all his creation.

"I'm who I need to be for Serena and Cayden, and that's something I'm proud of. Prouder than anything I've ever done, in fact."

I hated how I had to defend being a decent man to my wife and my son to this bastard.

He twisted his expression into one of disgust. "We all have our choices to make, Ryder. In the end, we'll have to pay for them, one way or another."

Whatever I'd hoped to do with this meeting had gone horribly off-track, so I tried to direct the conversation back to what choices we'd both made in the hopes of getting him to admit some of his misdeeds.

"Do you really believe that, Robert? We've done some horrible things in the past few years."

He stared across the desk at me for a moment and then nodded. "That we have. That we have. If I was a religious man, I'd say things aren't looking too good for the afterlife for us. Thankfully, I'm not, so I don't worry about things like that. But it seems like you've grown a soul now. How's that working for you?"

"I always had a soul. I just put it aside for a while to do what you ordered."

He didn't take the bait and simply smiled. "I like these little visits. Next time, bring that grandson of mine with you, if you can pry him away from his mother, that is."

Every time he talked about Serena it was nastier and nastier. My need to defend her overwhelmed my need to do what the FBI wanted, and I said, "Serena's a good mother to Cayden. Why you can't see that I don't understand. But then again, you can't seem to understand why bringing Kitty here upsets her either."

Narrowing his eyes to angry slits, he asked, "Is this still my home? Do I not get to say who can live here?"

I couldn't sit there with him anymore. The combination of his temper and mine was destined to end in something ugly.

Standing from my seat, I shrugged. "It's still your home. Why worry about how one of your children feels about what you do?"

Robert stared up at me with a look that said he wanted this fight to escalate, no matter what I wanted. That smile of his spread slowly until he looked like a cat that had just eaten a canary. "Just one of my children? Having Kitty here doesn't bother you, Ryder?"

Disgusted by him and my inability to get him to say anything incriminating, I stopped censoring myself and said what I knew would hurt him. "I don't care. Feel free to have every woman I've fucked move in. Not all of them were as crazy about me as Kitty, but what the hell. Take your pick at my sloppy seconds. I have the woman I want."

I didn't wait for him to respond before I stormed out into the main hallway, happy to be away from him. Fuck Robert. And fuck his attempt to rattle me. I'd get him to admit what he was, and then he'd pay for everything he'd done, including being cruel to Serena.

Just before I reached the stairs, I saw Kitty. One quick glance at her overeager face told me she'd been waiting for me.

"Ryder, stop. I want to talk to you," she whispered as she looked across the hallway toward Robert's office with worry in her eyes.

"Why? What do we have to talk about?" I asked as I continued walking toward the stairs.

"Please. Just give me a minute. I want to talk to you about something."

The worry in her eyes morphed into desperation, and I wondered if Robert had done something to her or she knew something that might hurt Serena or the baby, so I reluctantly agreed. "Fine. Let's go to the kitchen."

I didn't bother waiting for her, but she hurried to keep up so by the time I turned around to face her, she was right up against me looking up at me with that same wish for more in her eyes than I ever wanted to give her or get from her.

Stepping back, I leaned against the island. "What did you want to talk about?"

She followed, taking a step toward me so she could cage me in with her body against the counter. "I know you probably don't want me here, but I'm glad I get the chance to see you again."

Her eyes opened wide and filled with hope for something that would never happen. She touched my forearm, but I pushed her away.

"Don't, Kitty. Whatever we were is over. I'm with Serena."

She frowned and fought back tears as she tried to touch me again and I moved away around her. "I love you, Ryder. I never stopped loving you. I know you cared about me once. You told me you did."

I shook my head in shock that she could have misunderstood my feelings for her so badly. "I never cared for you. I'm sorry. I don't mean to be harsh, but I never felt that way. You knew that."

"You did! You wouldn't have come over every week to see me and whenever I called you for help if you didn't care at least a little. I know you cared, Ryder."

Her pleading with me made my stomach turn. There she was in Robert's house sharing his bed and trying to get me back. It was sickening and stupid, and if she wasn't careful, she'd find herself in deep trouble she might not survive.

"Go back to Robert's townhouse, Kitty. I don't feel that for you. I never have. I'm sorry."

She moved to hug me and I pushed her away hard so she fell back into the counter. I didn't mean to do that, but I couldn't risk her finding out I was wearing a wire.

But even that didn't stop her pitiful begging. "Please, Ryder. Don't do this. I don't believe you feel nothing. I know how trapped this family can make a person feel. You feel that. I know you do. You don't love her. I don't believe you could. She can't know what you really are after growing up spoiled with that silver spoon in her mouth."

"Shut up, Kitty. You don't know what you're talking about. I love her. I always have. Even when I was with you, all that while I never stopped wishing I could be with her."

Even that blunt truth didn't make her stop wanting me. "She's not like you. You and I are the same kind of people. We understand what life's really like. I understand you, Ryder. You know that. You know she'll never be able to understand the man you are."

Everything about Kitty now disgusted me. From the heavy makeup on her eyes she was used to wearing when she danced to how her clothes fit too tightly even as she stood there in front of me in jeans and a t-shirt that would have looked incredible on Serena. I hated myself for ever being with her.

"You don't know anything about what kind of person I am. You never knew me. I was a body you enjoyed. That was it. You knew that. I never let you think it was anything more than just sex."

She clamped her hand onto my arm and held on tightly as she stared up at me with that horrible look of desperation she wore so naturally. "She doesn't know the real you either. If she knew all the things you've done, you'd see. She'd look down on you. That's how they are."

I tore my arm from her hold and backed up to get away from her. "See, that's where you're wrong. She knows all about who I am and everything I've done, and she still loves me."

"For how long? Do you really think she's so different from him? He goes through women like they're candy. How long do you think she's going to be happy with the life you give her here? He controls you as much as he controls me, Ryder. How long before she wants someone who can give her more than a room in someone else's house?"

"Don't. You don't know anything about what we have together."

"I belong with you! I've known that since that first night you saved me behind the club. You wouldn't have come back every time for two years if you didn't care, Ryder. You can lie to yourself all you want, but I know the truth. I see it in your eyes."

"I don't want you. How many times do I have to tell you that before you get it through your thick head? I don't want you! I've never wanted you. Not a single time when we were together. You weren't the one I wanted, Kitty. You never were."

I knew how cruel those words were, and if I'd ever cared at all about her, I wouldn't have been able to say them. But she was wrong. I loved Serena. I always had.

Finally, what I said sunk in, and Kitty staggered back until she hit the wall near the refrigerator. Hurt and upset, she started to cry.

"What's happened to you, Ryder? Where's the guy who was so kind whenever I needed him all those times?"

I didn't want to stand there anymore with her. We had nothing in common. We never had. Now it was just more obvious.

"Stay away from me and Serena. I won't tell you again, Kitty. Go back to his townhouse. That's where you belong."

"I don't want him. I want you. I always have," she sobbed.

"You're playing a dangerous game here, Kitty. Don't let him find out you don't want him, if you want to keep breathing. Whatever you're getting out of this, I hope it's worth it."

"I only agreed to move in because I knew you were here. I don't love him. How could I?"

Turning to look out into the hallway, I hoped to God I wouldn't see Robert there. "Kitty, get away from this house now. I don't know if he cares about you or not, but he doesn't take people playing games. You're out of your league with him. When he finds out you want someone other than him, you're going to get hurt."

"You really don't care about me, Ryder?"

I shook my head. "No. I've always loved Serena, Kitty. Take my advice and get away from here as quick as you can."

As I walked out into the hallway, I heard her begin to cry again. I didn't know what Robert was up to bringing her here because I doubted Kitty could ever lie well enough for him not to know how she felt about me. Whatever it was, she was going to get hurt.

My job was to make sure Serena and Cayden didn't get hurt too.

As I made my way back upstairs, I tried to figure out a way to get Robert to talk for the next time I went to see him. The FBI wasn't going to let me off the hook after this first attempt to get him to incriminate himself. I truly was trapped between the devil on one side and the deep blue sea on the other.

And neither one would give up until they got what they wanted out of me.

Chapter Nineteen

Serena

THE BEDROOM DOOR opened and Ryder stormed through, slamming it behind him. Stuffing his hand beneath his shirt, he ripped the wire off his skin. He tossed it onto the dresser, making it skid down the top into my perfume bottles that went crashing to the floor.

"It went as bad as it looks," he grumbled. "I'm beginning to wonder if I'm ever going to be able to give them what they want, but if I don't, they're going to send me to jail."

"There has to be a way," I said as Ryder sighed and sat down on the edge of the bed.

"I don't know. I'll have to figure out a way to get him to talk next time."

He ran his hand through his hair like he did when the stress got too much for him, so I knelt down in front of him and took his hands in mine. I dipped my head to kiss his knuckles and looked up to see him smiling down at me.

"I wanted this to be over. I really did."

"I know. It will be," I said quietly, trying to hide my disappointment.

But as I knelt there, a familiar and disgusting scent floated into my nose. I stood and shook my head to get rid of that cheap perfume smell.

"Why do you stink of her?" I snapped. "I thought you were going to talk to him alone."

A look of hatred crossed his face, and he bolted up from the bed. "I can't do this with you, Serena. Not now. I told you I don't give a fuck about her. I'm sorry he ever brought her here. I don't care about her. How many times do I have to tell people that before they believe me?"

I stood there staring in shock at him. Ryder never barked at me like that. I wanted to tell him I knew he never cared about her, even if my jealousy made it seem like I didn't believe it. It was just my insecurities that came out every time that putrid smell hit my nostrils.

Before I could say a word, he walked away to the bathroom and slammed the door shut behind him. I sat down on the bed feeling empty, like a part of me had been ripped away. I knew it was just a fight, but there was something else too.

We were beginning to crack from the pressure of everything we had to deal with here. If we didn't find a way out soon, I was afraid we might not make it through this.

I couldn't let that happen. Not after all we'd weathered just to get to this point.

Slowly, I opened the bathroom door just a crack and heard the shower running. God, he was a wonderful man. Even though he wanted to scream at me for being so ridiculous about her, he was in there washing away that smell because he knew it bothered me.

He stood leaning against the tile wall, his head bowed like in defeat as the water hit him and ran down his back. I watched through the glass shower door wishing I wasn't so foolish. Ryder had never been anything but wonderful to me, and how did I repay him for that?

With petty accusations based on nothing because I couldn't get past my jealousy of her because she'd had a part of him before me.

Stripping out of my clothes, I stood there as my gaze slid over his body, so hard and muscular, and I wanted nothing more than to make sure he knew how much I loved him and how much I hated when I made him feel this way.

I stepped into the shower and without a word, slipped my arms around his waist. Pressing my cheek to this back, I whispered, "I'm sorry. I don't know what's wrong with me."

Ryder didn't move, keeping his hands firmly planted on the wall in front of him and his head down. "There's nothing wrong with you, Serena," he said in a low voice full of anguish.

Water rolled down his back and over my face as I clung to him. I'd hoped he would respond to me as soon as I stepped into the shower, but he remained lost in his misery.

I slid my hands over his hard abs, loving the feel of him beneath my hands. "I didn't mean that I thought you were with her. I don't think that. I know I shouldn't be jealous of her, but I am. I don't know what to do about that."

He stayed silent for a long moment before turning around to face me. "Jealous of her? Why?" he asked, his expression pure confusion.

Admitting the truth made me feel so stupid. He'd saved me over and over, putting his life and his happiness on the line just for me so many times I couldn't count them anymore. For those things alone, I should have known how much Ryder loved me.

Looking up into his deep green eyes, I saw he truly had no idea why I could be jealous of her. In truth, I knew it was a small thing compared to all we'd been through, but I'd never been able to overcome those feelings of insecurity when it came to her.

"Because she got to have part of you before I did. She'll always have that."

He cradled my face in his strong hands and shook his head. "She never had any part of me. No part that matters, anyway. Whatever I did with her, it was my body, not my heart involved."

I hung my head in shame. "I'm sorry, Ryder. I don't want to feel like this. I don't. I know how much you love me. I've never doubted it. But then I think of you with her and everything I know goes out the window, leaving me wishing I'd never gone away for those two years."

"You had no choice. He sent you away. I'm sorry she makes you feel like this. I swear, Serena, it never meant anything to me. If I could go back and do things differently, I would. I'd find a way to get to Italy and we'd be there today living happily and eating spaghetti all the time."

I looked up at him and smiled at his silly joke. "Italy isn't all about pasta, you know."

"I know. I just wanted to see you happy again."

"I wish we were in Italy right now. You know that?"

He dipped his head and kissed me sweetly on the lips. "Me too. Anywhere but in this house."

The last thing I wanted to think about at that moment as we stood naked in each other's arms in the shower was this house and all the awful things that came with it. I kissed him back and ran my hands down his body until I felt the hard ridge of muscle near his hips. Trailing my fingertips over it, I palmed him and moaned into his mouth at the feel of his thick cock growing hard in my hand.

"I want to feel you inside me, Ryder."

Grinning, he slowly ran his tongue across his bottom lip. "Your wish is my command, my lady."

He lifted me by my waist, and I wrapped my legs around his body, my water-slick skin gliding against his sides. His hands slid down to cup my ass as he kissed my neck and groaned, "It's always been you, Serena. Only you."

I knew that, even though it thrilled me each time he said it. I loved hearing the man I adored tell me he'd loved me even when I was gone from his life for all that time.

Smoothing his hair back off his face, I marveled at how lucky I was to have this man care about me. Not only was he gorgeous and had a great body, but underneath that beautiful outside beat the heart of a loyal and devoted man who loved me. I didn't know if I deserved him, but I never wanted to know what life was like without him.

"I love you, Ryder. You're the only man I ever want."

He pushed his hips forward and his hands squeezed my flesh as his cock slid into me until there was nothing separating us. My hands clung to his neck and he began to pump into me, slowly at first with long, teasing movements in and out of my body that sent waves of pleasure rolling over every inch of me.

I dug my heels into his back to urge him for more. More of his cock inside me. More of the guttural sounds that filled my ears he made every time he filled me to the hilt. More of his mouth on me.

More of him.

He eased me back toward the wall, and I felt the cool tile press against my skin as the heat of the water beating down on us warmed every part it hit. The combination mixed with the sensations he produced in me as he fucked me and began to overwhelm me with desire.

I bucked against him, wanting to ride every rock hard bit of his cock. Inch by incredible inch filled me and then left me needing more. Over and over, I pulled him back into me, never wanting to be empty of him again.

"That's it, baby. Ride my cock just like that," he groaned into my ear. "I love how you feel around me."

"Oh…God…Don't stop…God, don't stop…" I moaned as he began to jackhammer into me.

He planted his hands on the wall on either side of my head and let his hips set the pace, stabbing his cock in and out. I scratched my nails across the back of his neck, eliciting a low growl from him that sounded like it came from deep inside him somewhere.

"Fuck…hold on, baby. I'm almost there."

I wanted to hold on as he said to, but my release rushed over me and I buried my teeth in his shoulder as I came hard, my hips rolling to feel him against my clit and extend the exquisite feeling of coming. Ryder moaned about my pussy milking his cock, and then a few seconds later, his body stilled and he came inside me as he sagged against the wall.

Smoothing my hand down the back of his head, I took a deep breath and slowly let it out, enjoying the feel of us still joined together as the water rolled over us. He didn't smell like her anymore.

He smelled like him. Masculine. Ryder.

"My legs are starting to feel like jelly," he said quietly as he leaned back away from me. "I don't know if it's the heat from the shower or the fact that I might have nearly blacked out when I came, but that might have been the best shower sex we ever had."

"Nearly blacked out? Who knew sex could be so dangerous for you?" I asked with a giggle.

"I like to live on the edge," he said with that genuine smile he wore when he was feeling playful.

"One of the million reasons why I love you. Now let me down since I think my legs are going numb."

He set me down on my feet and kissed me softly on the lips. "Just a million. I better get working on that. I've got at least two million reasons why I love you."

"I love when you're cute. When you're like this, you're so relaxed and it's like the rest of the world doesn't exist."

Ryder pressed his forehead to mine and smiled. "When we're together like that, nothing exists but you, Serena. That's how it's always been with us from that first night you came to my room."

I pulled him to me and held him tightly, never wanting to let him go. "Tell me we won't forget that ever. Tell me we won't let everything around us make us forget how much we love being with each other."

"We won't. Some things you just can't forget."

He was right. Someday, all the bad would fade away into the distance, leaving only the memories of those nights when we lay together talking and all the happiness we'd found once I returned from Italy.

We wouldn't forget because those times were who we really were. Two people crazy, madly, and completely in love.

I LAY WRAPPED in his arms, safe from all that could hurt us. If only we could never have to leave that room.

"He's not going to stop lording his power over us, Serena. You know that like I do," Ryder whispered into the darkness.

"I know. I've known it since the night he sent me away to Italy."

He sighed above me. "If only I had gotten us away when we had the chance."

I didn't know which time he meant, but it didn't matter. I knew he regretted every time we didn't leave this place.

"How are we going to live like this, Ryder? We can't for much longer."

He remained silent for a long time before he said, "Tonight, he taunted me about turning me in to the police for what happened with that fighter up in West Virginia."

Nothing my father did surprised me anymore. I'd thought Ryder was his favorite, not only among his employees but among those of us he called his children. Now that seemed long in the past. If he could threaten him with going to jail for that fight, what else would he do to him?

Ryder pressed a kiss to the top of my head and held me close. "I won't let him hurt you or Cayden. I promise you that."

I looked up at him and wondered why he hadn't included himself in that promise. "What about you? I don't want him hurting you either. You won't be able to protect us if you're not here, and I worry someday soon he's going to make that happen."

He shook his head like what I said wasn't even a possibility, but I saw in the dim light the fear in his eyes. "I swore I'd protect you, Serena. I won't let him tear us apart, no matter what I have to do."

"I want you to swear something else to me."

"Anything."

"Swear that no matter what you do, you remember the man you are, Ryder. You're a good man. I've never doubted you would protect me and protect our son, but I can't stand the idea that if he backs you into a corner, that you'll be tormented for the rest of your life by what you had to do. You don't deserve that."

He looked down at me and his mouth turned down into a frown. "I never wanted to be his son or his favorite. I just wanted to live. Then when I fell in love with you, I just wanted to be happy with you in my life. I don't know why, but he doesn't seem to want me to have either a life or happiness. If it comes down to me or him, I'm going to do what I have to so at the end of the day, I have you and Cayden and a chance for a happy life."

I rested my head on his chest over his heart. Closing my eyes, I listened to the rhythm of its beating and prayed to God my father wouldn't force Ryder to fight for that life we wanted. We'd already fought so much. There was no way we would give up now.

So my father had a choice. Accept us together and leave us alone or find out just how much a man will do for the life he's dreamed of.

Sadly, I knew what my father would do. He'd do what he'd always done.

But this time, it wouldn't end up like it always had. This time he'd lose.

Chapter Twenty

Ryder

THE THREE OF US sat in the grass at the back of the garden near where the rose bush Alita planted still stood. Cayden giggled, kicking his legs out each time Serena tickled him, and she laughed along with him. Every day after work I wanted to come out here and enjoy this with them, but it seemed like by the time I finished my time sitting in that room working security for the estate, all I could think of was going back to either our bedroom or Cayden's nursery and hiding out.

That had become our lives. Whether we wanted to admit it or not, we were as good as prisoners there in that house.

I couldn't stand the thought of my son growing up like Serena had. For all the bad I'd seen after my parents died, I had good memories of a life before then that included picnics and vacations and times full of love and warmth.

Cayden and Serena deserved that kind of life, and I wanted to give it to them.

She pressed her lips to his bare belly and blew out against his skin. "Who's Mommy's big boy? Is it Cayden?"

He giggled at the feel of her tickling him and smiled up at her like he'd never been happier before that moment. She repeated the whole thing once more, and he burst out laughing again.

I could watch them for the rest of my life and never get tired of seeing them interact like that.

Turning to look at me, Serena reached out and tickled my ribs. "Daddy needs to laugh too. Doesn't he, Cayden?"

"I just like seeing you two go at it," I said, tucking her hair behind her ear. "I like it back here."

Serena looked around and nodded. "I know why my mother liked it back here. It doesn't even feel like we're still on the estate."

My phone vibrated in my pocket, interrupting the happiness I'd enjoyed for the past half hour. Instantly, my body tensed. I knew who it was. Why he felt the need to bother me now I had no idea. He probably saw me walking out here after I left the security room.

Looking down at where my phone continued to vibrate, Serena shook her head. "Don't answer it. Let it go until later. He can wait until we're done out here, can't he?"

I knew what would happen if I didn't answer.

He'd come find me and ruin our time together. I didn't want another scene between Serena and him over the baby. Better for me to just answer the damn call and find out what he wanted.

"You don't want him walking out here, do you? Because you know that's what he'll do," I said as I fished the phone out of my pocket.

One look at the name on the screen told me I'd been right. Robert. Standing, I walked away from her and the baby. I answered the call and before I could say a word, he began talking.

"Ryder, I need you to come down to the warehouse tonight at seven. I've got a project you're going to help me with."

Surprised that he wanted me to do anything with him since he had his men for things like this, I said, "Okay. What's the project?"

"I'll tell you when you get there."

"Why do you need me? If it has something to do with The Pit, why not talk to Floyd?"

"Floyd's dead. That means you're up."

My breath caught in my chest as the news that Floyd was gone too settled into my brain. Had he gotten rid of him because of what he'd done to help me with fighting behind his back? That had ended months ago. Why wait until now to do something?

"Dead? What happened?"

"They found him dead at his apartment.

Someone slit his throat from ear to ear and left him to bleed out alone in that dingy one room hellhole he called home."

"Jesus. Why?"

"We live in a dangerous world, son," Robert answered blithely.

I knew who was responsible for Floyd's murder, but I couldn't escape the fact that if he hadn't gone out on a limb to help me make money then, he might still be alive today.

"Yeah, I guess we do," I croaked out as my emotions began to get the best of me.

"Well, time to put the past behind you, son."

His chipper way of dismissing the life and death of someone he'd known for years bothered me. Something else seemed wrong too. Why have me go to the warehouse at all? My job now was security for the estate. He'd made that perfectly clear every time I asked about anything that didn't have to do with that.

"Why not have one of your guys do whatever you want me to do there? Aren't they supposed to take care of those kinds of things?"

The phone went silent for a long moment before he answered, "No one knows the fight scene better than you do, Ryder. I want your opinion on some improvements I plan to make to the building. Now meet me there at seven. Understand?"

"Okay. Seven then."

I ended the call and stuffed the phone back into my pocket. Turning around, I saw Serena waited to hear what he wanted. I didn't believe the story about him wanting to make improvements to the warehouse, but I knew she'd worry if she thought I suspected something, so I forced a casual expression and smiled.

"What did he want? You don't look unhappy, so that's something, right?" she asked in a hopeful voice.

"He wants my help with something Floyd was doing for him a few months ago," I said, forcing myself to smile even as my emotions about his death threatened to ruin my whole act.

"Did I hear you say he wants you to go to the warehouse? Is he expecting you to fight again?"

The mere thought of it made my stomach twist into a tight knot. After what I did to that fighter in West Virginia, I never wanted to lay my hands on another person like that for the rest of my life.

"No. Trust me, he doesn't want that. I'm sure it will be more of a hassle than anything else. He seems to find any reason he can to be a pain in my ass lately."

Serena nodded, as if she believed my idea. "He'll probably have her there with him too. Maybe Cayden and I can come with you."

I sat back down in the grass next to Cayden and kissed her. "No way is my son going anywhere near that place. I don't want you there either. You have nothing to worry about when it comes to her."

She smiled, but she was worried. I could tell.

"I know. I just figured we could be there for moral support."

"There's nothing moral about him or her, so I'm not sure any kind of support can help."

Serena grabbed my hand and squeezed it tightly. "I just worry, Ryder. I don't like it when he makes you run these errands for him. I don't trust him."

"I don't either, so don't worry. My guard is up already. I'll be fine. Just keep Cayden in our room until I get back."

Her expression darkened at my suggestion. "Why? Can't I just hang out with him in the nursery?"

"There's no lock on the nursery door, so no. I want you two in our room tonight."

Now fear settled into her eyes. "Why? Did he say he was going to do something with the baby?"

Pulling her close, I held her as she began to shake at the very thought of Robert taking our son. I didn't think he would, to be honest, but everything about his wanting me to come to the warehouse tonight felt wrong, so I didn't want to take any chances.

"No, everything's okay. I just want you two there when I get back. That's all. This way he'll be awake when I get home."

She looked up at me, searching my eyes for the truth I hoped wasn't in them. "That's it? Are you sure?"

"That's it. Sometimes it's just easier to have everyone you love all in one place."

Cayden began to cry, diverting Serena's attention for the moment, so she picked him up and placed him in the stroller. As we walked back to the house to get him ready for dinner, I hoped what I was sensing in my gut about tonight was wrong.

But no matter why Robert wanted me at the warehouse, I'd be ready.

✧　✧　✧

I SLID OPEN the metal door and stepped into the main part of the warehouse where fights were held. Looking around, I saw no one. No Robert or Kitty. None of his men either. Just that old, rusty metal folding chair I'd kept in what used to be my home when I lived here.

A light in Floyd's old office flickered at the other side of the room, so I made my way toward it, avoiding the broken pieces of concrete floor, and just before I reached the doorway, I stopped to check my gun tucked into the back of my pants.

Whatever Robert had planned, I had something planned too.

"You and the lurking, son. I have to think this is my daughter's influence on you since you never did it before you and she got together."

His mention of Serena once again in a negative way made me grit my teeth so I wouldn't say anything back. Instead, I kept my mouth shut and looked around the corner to see him sitting on top of Floyd's old desk. The old, possessed chair sat discarded in the corner, so I wouldn't get to enjoy seeing Robert tossed onto his ass tonight.

Too bad.

"Slumming it these days, Robert? If we were going to meet in an office, why didn't we just do it at the house where at least we might not be in danger of getting tetanus?" I asked, still wondering why we were at this place at all.

He waved his hand for me to come in. "Join me in our old friend's office. I'd turn on another light so you could see better, but I'm afraid good old Floyd didn't seem to be very interested in seeing much in here."

I stepped into the tiny office and my body stiffened as memories of Floyd came rushing back. I'd thought that crazy chair would be the end of him. Fuck, I was so naïve.

Robert pointed toward the corner of the room

and that old chair. "Feel free to pull up a seat. I want to talk to you before we begin."

"No, thanks. I'll stand."

"As you wish. How does it feel to be back here, son? You spent a lot of time in this place."

I didn't want him to have the satisfaction of knowing how terrible being there in Floyd's old office made me feel. Memories of him flooded my mind as I stood there, each one more painful than the last now that he was gone.

Shrugging, I looked around as if the place meant nothing to me. "I can't say it feels like anything, to be honest. I'm more interested in what you got me down here for. I'm sure you already have a new guy to do Floyd's job."

Robert sighed. "I do, but I don't know if he's going to work out. So I'm in the market for a new man, so to speak. I thought you'd be perfect for the job. I know you're going stir crazy sitting in front of those monitors all day and listening to Johnson and his fish tales. I think getting you out of the house will do us all some good."

"Do us all some good?" I repeated, struck by the way he'd worded that.

I didn't want to be his new Floyd and have to go find desperate kids to fight for him. My fighting days were over, and that included arranging them so he could benefit from the blood, sweat, and tears of fighters like me.

He nodded and pointed toward the door. "Let's go out to what you guys call The Pit and talk."

My gut said something was wrong. Would I step out of that office and get my head blown off by one of his men? I knew how Robert worked. He didn't do the dirty work. He had others who took care of that.

But he didn't wait for me and left first, so I followed him as my senses went on red alert. I wanted to believe my paranoia had gotten the best of me and he really did just want to talk about offering me Floyd's old job, but I knew better.

Walking past the metal folding chair, he motioned for me to sit down as he went to turn on the lights. "Take a seat, son."

I sat down this time and watched him walk toward me. We'd been here before—him standing over me as I sat waiting to hear the next thing that came out of his mouth.

"Do you remember the first time I met you right here in this building? Did you know that I made a fortune off you when you fought? I saw you when you won your first fight, and from that point on, I bet on you every time. Nearly twenty straight wins. I've never made more on any fighter, and that's saying something."

"I guessed you did," I said as he stopped directly in front of me.

"And then there was that last fight right after I caught you and my daughter together. I made a good bit of money that time too."

Staring up at him, I struggled to keep my emotions in check as his admission that he'd bet against me when he put me up against that fucking behemoth rolled through my brain. He wanted to get a rise out of me, but I wasn't going to give it to him.

"You know, you really were my favorite. Still are, if I'm being honest. I meant it when I said you were my adopted son. Then again, it's family that can hurt you the most more often than not. Right, son?"

I didn't know how to answer that question. Nobody knew how to hurt his family more than Robert, but he seemed to be referring more to my hurting him than his hurting his children and me.

His arm jerked behind him and suddenly I saw a gun pointed down at me. "I know all about what you've been up to with the FBI. You didn't think I'd figure it out? I figured it out with your friend Jesse before you too."

Terror raced through me, making my mouth go dry. "I didn't know what you'd figure out. Did you intentionally send me to get rid of him that night because you found out he was working with the FBI?"

Robert pursed his lips. "Kill two birds with one stone, although because of you the other bird had to wait a bit."

So Jesse has been working with the FBI against him.

"I didn't have a choice."

"I think I can say the same thing. I just want you to know a few things before I say goodbye."

His voice caught on the word goodbye. Circling around me, he grabbed my gun before I had the chance to pull it on him and even the odds, leaving me at his mercy.

When he came back around to stand in front of me again, he had a gun in each hand and both aimed at me. "I might not be a young buck like you, but I still know all the tricks."

"They came to me and threatened to have the cops get me for what happened in West Virginia, Robert. I couldn't let that happen to Serena and Cayden."

He winced, like something I said hurt him. "And does my daughter know what you were doing with the FBI?"

I nodded. "She knows."

"And just like that her loyalties to her father are replaced by loyalty to you," he said with a disgusted sneer.

His ability to be ignorant to how he'd treated her amazed me. "How can you expect her to be loyal to you at all? You pretty much set this in motion with every time you treated her like shit, Robert. Just since I came into the picture, you exiled her to another continent away from the only home she ever knew, brought her back just to imprison her in that home, married her off to a man she didn't love, beat me senseless for protecting her, and killed her mother. And just recently, you brought Kitty to the house to live. What did you expect?"

"I'm guessing you're the reason she left the other night," he said in a low voice.

The news that Kitty had moved out surprised me. "I have no idea why she left. Maybe she realized how shitty a thing it was to be there around Serena and me. Then again, for someone who would kill his daughters' mother, what you did with Kitty was nothing."

Staring past me, he got a faraway look in his eyes, and I expected to hear him claim he didn't kill Alita. Not that I'd believe him. I knew he did it.

But instead he said, "Those aren't the reasons why my daughter so willingly turned against me."

"I don't know what made her do it, Robert. I just know you terrify and upset her, now more than ever since Cayden came along. I think she worries you're going to take him away and make him like you."

He shook his head. "No, that's not it. Did she ever tell you about when she was kidnapped as a little girl? She was only around seven years old."

"Yeah. It's the reason she hates shoes and why you brought her home to be taught there because she was so traumatized by the whole thing."

He stared down at me and shook his head again, his mouth stretching to a thin line across his face. "It never happened."

"What do you mean? Don't bother telling me that Serena's a liar because I know better."

"It never happened. Everything she thinks happened is a false memory. I had to do something because she overreacted and I couldn't have her telling anyone. I'd gotten rid of her mother and I'd convinced her sister she couldn't be believed, but I didn't think she'd react that way. When she did, I had to come up with something fast. So that's what I did."

I'd never seen Robert look like this. His face twisted into a strange expression that looked like a mix between fear and satisfaction.

"What are you talking about? Are you saying you had your own daughter kidnapped? Why?" I asked, horrified at even the thought of someone doing that to their child.

"I didn't expect her to react that way. I was her father, after all. I'd tucked her into bed every night after her mother left. But she started crying and I hadn't even done much of anything, but I couldn't get her to stop crying. So I had to think fast and come up with something believable."

My mind whirled with confusion. What the fuck was he saying?

"Why would she cry, Robert? What did you do to make her cry like that?" I asked, unsure I wanted the answer.

"I've always loved Serena more. She was my favorite of the two of them. She'd sit on my lap and play with my tie with her little fingers. I was never happier than when she was next to me."

No.

He couldn't be saying what I thought he was saying.

But he kept talking, like he needed me to know his darkest secret before he killed me.

"She was crying and I didn't know what to do, so I had someone take her for a few days and they made sure she remembered only the kidnapping. But then her teacher told me she kept talking about it to the other students at school and suggested she needed professional help. I couldn't risk her saying anything to anyone, so I brought her home to be tutored there."

"Are you fucking saying you did something to her that night? Something a father shouldn't do, Robert? Is that what you're fucking telling me?" I asked as my heart began to pound so loud I wasn't sure I'd be able to hear his answer because of sound of the beating in my ears.

"I loved her like I'd never loved anyone else in the world. I'd never felt that way for anyone before Serena. I didn't dare try again, though, because I couldn't just have her kidnapped again."

Lost in his thoughts, he looked like he didn't even know I was still there, so I took the chance and charged him. He fell to the ground easily, the guns skidding across the concrete as his hands hit. He stared up at me in surprise, and for a moment, I just looked down at him, finally knowing what kind of monster he really was at last.

Then something in my brain snapped as the horrible image of him abusing Serena all those years ago settled into my mind, and I cocked my arm back like I would with anyone I'd taken to the ground in a fight. I pushed my fist forward with all I had, slamming into his face so hard I heard his cheekbone crack.

"You fucking bastard! How could you do that to her?" I screamed over and over as I hit him harder than I'd ever hit any fighter I'd faced.

Once I started, I couldn't stop, even if I wanted to. He raised his hands to try to defend himself the first few times, but it was no use. I pounded his face over and over for what he'd done to Serena. For all the abuse she'd suffered over the years at the hands of a monster who claimed to love her most.

I beat him with my bare hands until I couldn't feel anything in them anymore. My bloody and raw knuckles landed onto his face until he was unrecognizable. I didn't even know if he was still alive when I sat back on my heels, exhausted and still so full of rage I didn't know what to do with myself as tears streamed down my face.

He lay there motionless, and I didn't care if I'd killed him.

Whatever I did to him was nothing compared to what he'd done to her.

Chapter Twenty-One

Serena

THE BEDROOM DOOR opened and Ryder walked in and said nothing as he picked up Cayden. Holding him to his chest, he kissed him and looked over at me.

"I need to take a shower, but I needed to see this little guy and you more."

His knuckles looked like he'd spent the last hour sparring with a cinder block. I scanned his face but saw no cuts or bruises, but he didn't look right. Something was definitely wrong.

I hurried over to him, and he put his arm around me. "Are you okay, Ryder? You look awful. What happened? Did my father make you fight someone? I sat here the whole time worried he'd spring that on you."

Shaking his head, he frowned. "I'm okay. He had a surprise for me, but I'm fine now. I want you to take Cayden to his crib and put him down for the night. I need to talk to you."

My blood ran cold at the seriousness of his tone.

"Why? What's wrong? What did he do?"

He kissed me and then kissed the baby. "Just take him and come back, okay? It's all going to be fine. I promise."

I did as he said and found him coming out of the shower when I returned. A quick study of his body told me whatever had caused the cuts on his knuckles hadn't touched him anywhere else.

He rubbed a towel over his wet hair and then looked up at me with an expression that made my heart sink. I'd only seen fear in his eyes once or twice before, but never like this.

"What is it, Ryder? What happened? He can't send you away, right? We're married. Even he can't change that."

"It's not that," he said, stepping forward to kiss me softly on the lips.

"Then what is it? You're scaring me. I've never seen you like this."

He gently pressed his hands against my cheeks and stared into my eyes. "I have to tell you something."

I covered his hands with mine and felt like my entire world was falling apart as I stood there looking up at him. "What? What is it, Ryder?"

"I did it. I didn't mean to. I didn't go there to do that, but he started talking about…"

Shaking his head, he slid his hands from my face

and pulled me into him. "I'm sorry. He's dead, Serena."

Dead? I stood there in his arms as the news that my father was gone settled into my mind. I'd thought about life after him so many times, but that had always been something that might happen at some point in the future when he grew old and finally left this world.

But now Ryder was saying he was dead.

I leaned back away from him and stared up at him in disbelief. "Dead? He's really gone?"

"I didn't go there to do that, Serena. He pulled a gun on me. He got me there to kill me."

"Why?"

Ryder hung his head. "He knew all about me talking to the FBI. He wasn't going to just let that kind of betrayal go."

I pressed a kiss onto his still wet hair and whispered, "What now? Are you going to be arrested? It was self-defense, right? They won't put you in jail for that. You didn't have a choice. You have the right to defend yourself."

With each word, my voice pitched higher as my panic began to take over. My father couldn't win. Ryder didn't deserve to pay for just defending himself.

He lifted his head and tried to smile. "I don't know what's going to happen, Serena. I don't know if anyone is going to believe it was self-defense since all I have are some busted knuckles and he's…"

I watched as he couldn't even say the word. Dead. I knew I should have been sad. This was my father and he was gone, but I didn't even feel like crying. After all I'd been through, I didn't have any more tears for him.

All I felt was relief.

And complete terror at the thought that Ryder would be put away for life after all we'd gone through at the hands of my father.

"I won't let them take you away. They can't. Not after all we've been through because of him, Ryder. This can't happen. He can't win in the end. I won't let him!"

He held me by my shoulders as I began to sob. "I'm not afraid of paying for what I did. He had it coming and it was self-defense, but I'm not sure anyone's going to believe that. I'm going to stay here with you and hold you in my arms, and when Cayden wakes up, we're going to go into his room and spend however long we want with him. If they come for me, they come. I told you I'd protect you and our son, and that's what I did."

"But I can't stand the idea that after everything we've been through that he's going to win in the end."

Taking my hand in his, he brought it to his lips

and kissed my fingers. "Whatever happens, you're safe now. Whether I'm here or not, you won't have to worry anymore."

I wrapped my arms around him and clung to his neck, afraid at any moment I'd hear a knock on the door and the police would be there to take him away forever. "Don't talk like that! I don't want to even think about you not being here, Ryder. Cayden and I need you!"

"It's going to be okay. I promise. Just believe me. You're safe now."

We lay together silently for hours until Cayden's cries came through the baby monitor, and then the two of us walked down to his nursery. Ryder sat at my feet as the baby fed, watching like it might be the last time he saw the action that had been common-place before. I wanted to burst into tears, but I didn't because if this was the last night we all had together, it was going to be the way we always dreamed life would be.

Happy and content.

When we woke up in the morning, we warily walked down to the kitchen, the two of us expecting at any moment to hear that knock on the door.

But it didn't come.

Day after day, we continued to live like we always had, except the fear that at some point someone would come looking for Ryder hung over our heads. I did as he suggested and reported my father missing and told Janelle about him not coming home. I'd expected the police to launch a major investigation like they did on TV when important people went missing, but all they did was take my information and assured me they would be in touch when they had any news to tell me. Janelle barely acknowledged him being missing. I'd expected her to be upset, but she never even called back after I told her.

Every night I asked Ryder why no one seemed to miss my father. None of his men came to the main house, and by the time a week had passed without any sign of my father's return, they had all left and I began to wonder if anyone cared at all that he seemed to have just disappeared.

And then one day nearly two weeks after Ryder came home that night with bloody knuckles, the police came to the front door. I answered it and felt every ounce of my strength evaporate when I looked out and saw the two men standing in their dark blue uniforms.

"Officers?"

"Miss, we're here to speak to a relative of Robert Erickson's. Are you his daughter?" one officer asked in a grave voice.

"Yes," I answered, my mouth bone dry.

"May we come in?"

The last thing I wanted to do was let the police in, but I knew I didn't have a choice. Stepping back out of the way, I put on my biggest smile.

"Sure. Please come in."

My hands shook as I closed the door behind them, and when I turned to face them, I saw not the authoritarian expressions I'd expected but sympathetic ones. The man who spoke before took a deep breath and said, "Miss, we're sorry to have to tell you this, but your father was found dead in the bay. He's been dead over a week."

I didn't have to playact at hearing the news. I'd bottled up my emotions since that night my father ordered Ryder to the warehouse, and now that he'd been found, I couldn't stop the tears from coming. Right there in front of the two officers, I sobbed uncontrollably, but not for the reason they thought.

They tried to be kind and expressed their condolences, but it all felt so surreal. I knew who had killed my father and I didn't blame him one bit. I knew very few people would understand why, and maybe both Ryder and I were bad people.

All I knew was I was finally free.

✧　✧　✧

JANELLE, CHARLES, RYDER, AND I sat around the dining table listening to my father's lawyer read his will. After a week of dealing with the business of his death, this one last detail remained. My sister eagerly waited to hear the financial details about what he had left her, and even though she and her husband hadn't lived together for months, he sat next to her very interested in his wife's family, for once.

Ryder and I held hands under the table as the lawyer began to get to who had been left what. The man pushed his glasses up his nose and stopped reading for a moment before he lifted his head and stared down the table at Janelle and me.

"Mr. Erickson left everything—his businesses, the estate, and all his holdings—to one person."

I looked across the table at her and smiled. "He always did like you best."

His favoritism of Janelle didn't bother me so much anymore. I never understood why, but I'd never been enough. Maybe I was too much like my mother.

My sister, always the humble one, grinned at her imminent windfall. "I won't throw you guys out, so don't worry. I'm nicer than that, Serena. I would never send my nephew out into the streets."

I squeezed Ryder's hand and bit my tongue. Nice had never been a word I'd thought of to describe Janelle.

"Thanks. It's nice to know we won't be homeless."

The lawyer cleared his throat, and we all directed

our attention to the head of the table to hear him say Janelle had gotten everything. He pushed his glasses up the bridge of his nose once more and began reading again.

"As I said, your father left everything to one person. Ryder Rhodes. Neither of you are mentioned anywhere in the will."

My mouth dropped open in shock, and out of the corner of my eye, I saw Janelle and her husband instantly become enraged. I don't know why I was surprised. I shouldn't have been. My father always wanted a son, and in Ryder that's what he'd gotten.

Janelle jumped up out of her seat and screamed, "Are you fucking kidding me? This stray he brought home gets everything? After all he did to make my life miserable, he left me nothing? Over my dead body!"

She stormed out, followed by her husband, leaving the three of us sitting there, and I couldn't help but laugh. Made her life miserable? She didn't have a clue.

"I'm sorry I had to be the bearer of bad news, Serena," the lawyer said in a truly sympathetic voice. "I know your father cared a great deal about you and your sister, even if it seems as if this will proves otherwise. He did make sure to include provisions to ensure that Janelle's house is paid in full."

"I'll make sure to tell her. She's a little bit

surprised, as you can tell."

The poor guy was just doing his job. It wasn't his fault my father had no use for females.

He finished reading the entire will and then left. Ryder sat silently beside me, still holding my hand under the table as he stared straight ahead like his brain hadn't processed the news that he was now a very wealthy man.

"So in the end, in death my father showed what was important to him in life," I said as I lifted our hands and rested them on the table in front of us.

He turned to look at me and shook his head. "I'm sorry. This isn't right. Not after what you went through all your life."

"My father never thought much of me or Janelle. We weren't sons. In you, he got the son he always wanted. And in the end, he got what he deserved."

"I think in his own twisted way he thought he was showing you love. I'd hoped that for once he'd do the right thing by you at the end," Ryder said sadly.

"Don't feel bad. It's okay."

He shook his head and his frown deepened. "It's not okay. Nothing he did to you was okay, Serena."

I smiled, knowing he was right. "I know. He made my life difficult on the best days, and he forced me to marry a man I didn't love. But he did one thing that I can't hate him for."

"What's that?"

"He brought you to me."

We walked out toward the stairs to go up to see our son, but a knock on the front door stopped us. Smiling, I joked, "Maybe it's the lawyer coming back to tell us you got something more."

Ryder rolled his eyes and shook his head as he made his way to the door. "I never wanted anything from him. You know that."

"I know. I was just trying to lighten the mood a little."

He opened the door, and I saw two men in dark suits standing outside. Ryder's entire body stiffened at the sight of them, so I hurried to join him and whoever they were.

One man smiled and said, "Ryder, we wanted to come out and let you know the case concerning Robert Erickson is closed."

I took Ryder's hand in mine and asked, "Honey, who are these men?"

Turning to look at me, he answered, "Serena, these men are from the FBI."

Fear tore through me that they weren't just there to let Ryder know the case against my father had been closed because of his death. Leveling my gaze on the two of them, I said, "How nice of you to come all the way out here to let us know. This has been a very difficult time for our family, so I hope you'll understand our need to be alone with our loved ones now."

The man who'd told Ryder the news smiled and nodded his head. "We certainly can understand, Mrs. Rhodes. I'm sorry to hear from the police that they don't think they're ever going to be able to bring the person responsible for your father's death to justice. I'm afraid this case may remain unsolved forever."

Ryder let out a sigh and smiled at the man. "Thank you for letting us know."

As they walked away back to their car, I closed the door. "So that's the FBI, huh? They seemed pretty nice."

"Let's just say they're nicer when they aren't blackmailing you."

As we made our way up to Cayden's nursery, I was sure that was true. I was also sure of something else. From now on, our lives were our own.

For me, it would be the first time ever that would be true.

Chapter Twenty-Two

Ryder

Three Years Later

"DADDY, I WANTED to stand next to you, but Mommy says I need to stand next to her. Can I stand next to you?" Cayden asked in his most serious voice.

I looked to my left to see Serena shifting our daughter from her right arm to her left before my gaze drifted down to the open spot between us where Cayden would stand. "If you stand where she wants you to, you'll still be next to me. You'll just be on the other side."

My answer perplexed him, and he drew in his eyebrows to show his unhappiness with it. We'd never get this picture taken if he kept arguing about where he'd stand, so I tousled his dark hair and gently moved him around to stand between his mother and me.

"Ryder, I'm not sure Alita is going to be able to be her sweet self if we don't get this show on the road," Serena said as our two-year-old daughter began to complain that she wanted to stand where Cayden was.

The photographer waiting across the room chuckled. "I want to make sure you all fit behind the desk. Maybe if your son stands on the other side it will be better because it will be more balanced."

Happy to hear someone agreed with his idea, Cayden ran behind my chair and stood on my right side. Looking up at his mother, he said, "See, Mommy. Even the camera man said I should stand over here."

Serena took a deep breath and closed her eyes as Alita began asking if she could stand next to Cayden. I had a feeling at any moment she would announce this whole photo shoot was over and march the children upstairs to their rooms.

"Enough! Cayden is standing over here, and Alita, you do as your mother says. Understand me?"

They both looked at me with big eyes, and I saw Serena smile for the first time since we all walked into the office. This was just supposed to be a few pictures for an article in American Entrepreneur about Erickson Industries, and in less than ten minutes it had turned into a three-ring circus.

I'd agreed to the shoot only if Serena and the children could be included because no article on the business would be right without them. I may have been the CEO of Erickson Industries, but I could never have done it without Serena and our kids.

In the time since Robert left everything to me, she and I had worked together to clean up every part of the company. Gone were the nightclubs, drugs, strippers, prostitutes, and underground fighting, and in their place were honest businesses that had made Erickson Industries into a multi-billion dollar a year business, all completely legal.

"Okay, if I can get everyone to look over here, let's see if we can make some magic here," the photographer said in a cheery voice that hid his impatience at having to wait for Serena and me to corral our kids.

"Remember to smile like we practiced," Serena said, subtly warning Cayden that sticking out his tongue as he had in every picture we'd ever taken of him was not allowed this time.

I gave her a sideways glance and tried not to laugh as Alita said in a sing-song voice, "Cheese!" as the photographer began shooting. After a few shots, he stopped and lowered his camera.

"Mrs. Rhodes, you don't have any shoes on. Do you want me to stop while you go put them on?"

I looked over at Serena and saw her shake her head and smile as she sweetly explained, "No. I don't wear shoes if I don't have to, and right now, I don't have to."

Fifteen minutes later, he had his shots and the

kids ran outside to play on the porch.

"Be sure to stay off the stairs, and Cayden, watch your sister," Serena yelled after them.

The photographer smiled as he packed up his gear. "You have a nice family there."

I couldn't have agreed more. Serena and I thanked him as he left, and she kissed me sweetly on the cheek. "That was as difficult as I worried it would be."

"Here, sit down," I said as I offered her the chair. "You shouldn't be standing. You should have been the one who was sitting behind the desk."

She smiled and didn't argue with me before taking my seat. "You're the CEO of Erickson Industries, Ryder. It doesn't matter that I'm pregnant. Readers expect you to be sitting behind the desk in your office."

Rolling my eyes, I leaned down and kissed her. "You're as much the CEO as I am, Serena. More, if we're being honest since you're an Erickson. And this is our office in our house, remember?"

She slid her hands over her very pregnant belly. "My name is Serena Rhodes. It has been for years. That's why our kids are named Cayden Rhodes and Alita Rhodes, and whatever this child turns out to be will have the last name Rhodes."

"Well, you were originally an Erickson is what I meant."

Smiling, she looked up at me. "I like being a Rhodes better. And I like our house with the white picket fence much better than where we used to live."

"Well, Mrs. Rhodes, that photo shoot really didn't go too badly, did it? Not too much of a disaster," I said with a chuckle as I sat down in the black chair in front of the desk.

"Yeah, not too much. I'm dreading the idea of another one when we have three kids. We'll be outnumbered then. That's a disaster waiting to happen."

"Maybe we can ask Janelle to babysit that day."

Serena thought about my suggestion and nodded. "That could work. She does love hanging out with the kids. I just hope she doesn't bring that boyfriend of hers with her. I'm not sure about him."

Once he realized there would be no money from Robert's will, Charles divorced Janelle to run off with his mistress, leaving Serena's sister to finally try to find a normal life not dictated by Robert or his handpicked choice for a husband. Her decision was to get involved with the drummer from some rock band in Virginia and move in with him less than a month after they met at some bar one night.

She'd only brought him around a few times since they got together, and as far as I could tell, he seemed like a decent guy. I wasn't sure about the eighties throwback look he had with the long hair, but the conversations I'd had with him hadn't been too bad. He was definitely better than that stick-in-the-mud Charles she'd been with first.

"Mitch isn't too bad. I mean, the ripped jeans thing when he's not playing seems a little weird, but he's all right."

Serena twisted her face and shrugged. "I guess. Janelle seems to be crazy about him. Not that she's ever been the best judge of character."

"She likes our kids, and if I remember correctly, she liked me enough to practically proposition me way back when," I joked, unable to stop myself from laughing.

Rolling her eyes, Serena stood from her chair and came around the desk to sit on my lap. "You're not her type. Your hair is too short."

I rested my hand on her belly and leaned down to talk to our unborn child. "Do you hear your mother, little one?"

"She hears me and she agrees. You'd be terrible with her Aunt Janelle. Like oil and water."

Looking up at her, I smiled. "She was never the sister I wanted anyway. I liked the one who never wore shoes."

Serena lifted her tanned legs into the air and wiggled her toes with their pink painted nails. "Still doesn't. Some things stay with you forever. I'm always going to be a no-shoe girl."

The memory of what Robert told me that last night in the warehouse ran through my head, and I hugged her close to me. "I love that no-shoe girl. Always have."

She kissed me sweetly and giggled in that way that never failed to charm me. "And I've always loved you, but this no-shoe girl has to go get our kids before they lay waste to the place. I haven't heard a peep from them in almost five minutes, which tells me we're all in danger."

I helped her ease off my lap and stood up to follow her. "Tell them if they're good we'll go to the zoo this afternoon. That should help."

Turning around, she backed out the office door as she blew me a kiss. "They're going to hold you to that, you know. Don't say it if you don't mean it."

"I mean it. Tell them we'll leave early enough to get lunch on the way and then it's off to the zoo."

She headed outside to tell the kids the good news, and I heard them squeal with delight through the office window. Surprising them never failed to make me happy, just like seeing Serena content in our life. It's why I'd happily sold the estate and moved us to this house in the mountains with the big yard and a picket fence we painted white.

In the nearly three years since Robert's death, I'd watched for any sign she remembered what he'd done to her. I'd met with doctors who specialized in repressed memories to find out what I should do if what happened ever came back to her, and I was ready if it ever did.

I prayed to God she never remembered what that monster did to her, but if she did, I'd be there like I always promised her I would be. From that night I found her in that bathtub bleeding to death, I swore I'd protect her. I hadn't always succeeded, but that didn't mean I wouldn't move heaven and earth to try.

Serena and I had weathered every storm, and if that ugliest storm came, we'd deal with it like we always had.

Together.

We'd dreamed of a future where we would be happy, and we'd fought tooth and nail to get it. We'd done horrible things and given up things other people would have clung to because they were worth millions, but to us, they were only reminders of what we'd had to suffer through to be together.

I'd lived with next to nothing and lived with more than any one man could ask for. None of it would mean anything without her. Like it had been right after we first met, I started each day happy to know she was in my life and went to sleep each night with her head on my shoulder.

And for the people who would say because of what I've done that I'm nothing more than a common criminal, I say this. Until you're willing to put your life on the line to protect someone, you don't know what you'd do for love. When it's real, that devotion you feel is worth any cost.

I don't lay awake every night anymore haunted by the things I did. All I can do is hope that the man I am now will someday make up for what I did when I was one of Robert's men. And if I can't, it won't be because I didn't try.

But I've never lost a minute of sleep over what I did to Robert.

"Ryder, are you ready to go? Our two animals want to go to the zoo to see the other animals," Serena yelled in the window from outside in the yard.

"I'll be out in a minute. Just let me change out of this suit."

This was the life we'd looked forward to for so long, and it was everything I'd ever dreamed it could be. Whatever I was as a fighter and whatever I would be as a businessman or a father, I was never more than when I was just the man who loved her. She called me her savior, but in truth, it was Serena who saved me. Before her, all I knew was how to fight.

Because of her, I knew how to love.

**CONTINUE READING TO CHECK OUT
ALL OF K.M.'S BOOKS
AND FIND YOUR NEXT GREAT READ!**

About the Author

K.M. Scott writes contemporary romance stories of sexy, intense, and unforgettable love. A New York Times and USA Today bestselling author, she's been in love with romance since reading her first romance novel in junior high (she was a very curious girl!). Under her Gabrielle Bisset name, she writes erotic paranormal and historical romance. She lives in Pennsylvania with a herd of animals and when she's not writing can be found reading or feeding her TV addiction.

Be sure to visit K.M.'s Facebook page at **facebook.com/kmscottauthor** for all the latest on her books, along with giveaways and other goodies! And to hear all the news on K.M. Scott books first, sign up for her newsletter today and be sure to visit her website at **www.kmscottbooks.com**.

Books by K.M. Scott:

If I Dream (Corrupted Love #1)
If You Fight (Corrupted Love #2)
If We Fall (Corrupted Love #3)

Crash Into Me (Heart of Stone #1)
Fall Into Me (Heart of Stone #2)
Give In To Me (Heart of Stone #3)
Heart of Stone Volume One Box Set
Ever After (Heart of Stone #4)
A Heart of Stone Christmas (Heart of Stone #5)
Unforgettable (Heart of Stone #6)
Unbreakable (Heart of Stone #7)
Heart of Stone Volume Two Box Set

Temptation (Club X #1)
Surrender (Club X #2)
Possession (Club X #3)
Satisfaction (Club X #4)
Acceptance (Club X #5)
The Complete Club X Series Box Set

SILK (Volume One)
SILK (Volume Two)
SILK (Volume Three)
SILK (Volume Four)
SILK Box Set

K.M.'S BOOKS ARE IN AUDIOBOOK TOO!

Books by Gabrielle Bisset:

Vampire Dreams Revamped (A Sons of Navarus Prequel)

Blood Avenged (Sons of Navarus #1)

Blood Betrayed (Sons of Navarus #2)

Longing (A Sons of Navarus Short Story)

Blood Spirit (Sons of Navarus #3)

The Deepest Cut (A Sons of Navarus Short Story)

Blood Prophecy (Sons of Navarus #4)

Blood Craving (Sons of Navarus #5)

Blood Eclipse (Sons of Navarus #6)

The Sons of Navarus Box Set #1

The Sons of Navarus Box Set #2

Stolen Destiny (Destined Ones Duology #1)

Destiny Redeemed (Destined Ones Duology #2)

Love's Master

Masquerade

The Victorian Erotic Romance Trilogy

www.ingramcontent.com/pod-product-compliance
Lightning Source LLC
Chambersburg PA
CBHW051639180726
48284CB00006B/1785